An emotional and gripping
psychological, family drama

K.L Loveley

Globeflower Books ™

An imprint of The Globeflower Agency Ltd
Rural Innovation Centre,
Kenilworth, Warwickshire, CV8 2LG.

www.globeflower.co.uk

This is a work of fiction. Any names or characters, businesses or places, events, or incidents, are fictitious. Local and public names are sometimes used for atmospheric purposes. Any resemblance to actual persons, living or dead, or actual events is purely coincidental.

Front cover photograph Copyright © Jaromír Chalabala

A CIP catalogue record of this book is available in the British Library

Love, Secrets, and Absolution/ K.L Loveley. -- 1st ed.

ISBN 9978-1-9998294-0-7

DEDICATION

I dedicate this book to my late father, G.W Oliver, himself a true poet at heart disguised as a miner. Also to all coal miners around the world who have and still work down the coal mines.

In addition, I dedicate this book to my fictional character *Alfie* and to everyone who is involved with the support and care of people with Asperger syndrome and associated conditions.

ACKNOWLEDGMENTS

I would like to offer a huge heartfelt thanks to Anna-Lisa, the founder of *The Globeflower Agency Ltd*, who has published my novel under their imprint *Globeflower Books*. From the very beginning, she has believed in my writing and has worked tirelessly on developing the novel. I found her suggestions and advice paramount in helping to create the final book.

I would also like to provide a big thank you to my talented and hardworking editor Emma Mitchell, who has been extremely professional and supportive throughout the publishing process. I thoroughly enjoy working with her and appreciated all the constructive feedback she provided to help me develop the novel.

When I first started writing the novel, I went to my local library and was provided useful information about the miners' strike from the librarian and local archivist, Anne Sewell. Thank you, Anne, your work is greatly appreciated.

Of course, as always, I thank my husband Michael for his love and support and to my family and friends who are always enquiring how my next novel is progressing. Last, but not least, thank you so much to the bloggers and reviewers who have done so much to help me see my work through fresh eyes, allowing a different perspective. Finally, thank you, readers. Without you, where would I be?

K.L Loveley

As the snowflakes fell, Grace shivered and instinctively stroked her baby bump. Last night's heavy snowfall was unusual for March and had taken everyone by surprise, including Grace, who was ill-prepared for the long walk to the doctor's surgery. Underneath her unbuttoned coat, she wore a thin cardigan and a maternity dress. Her swollen feet were uncomfortable in the boots she had squeezed them into. She sighed out loud. *It's going to be a cold and miserable trek to the baby clinic,* she thought.

As soon as Grace stepped into the doctor's surgery, the warm air hit her and she instantly became relaxed. She notified the receptionist of her presence and sat down. As she gazed around the small waiting room she acknowledged the other mums-to-be, all of whom were younger than her.

'Ayup, Grace. Not long now eh, till your baby is due,' one of the women said.

Just then, Grace experienced a sharp kick from her baby. She smiled and lovingly stroked her belly. 'Shouldn't be too long now,' she replied.

The midwife measured her bump to calculate the fundal height and advised that according to her calculations the due date was today. However, after completing a multitude of other examinations, the midwife declared with some trepidation that Grace wouldn't be giving birth just yet.

'Your baby is a stubborn one and definitely nowhere near ready to come. Ain't got its head engaged yet,' the midwife chortled.

Grace became frustrated and thought, *what did the midwife mean by "head not engaged?"*

As Grace set off home and waded through the snowy village, she kept thinking about this strange terminology. She was so engrossed in her thoughts, that she lost concentration and fell onto the wet, cold ground in an uncompromising position. Fortunately, one of her husband's work colleagues' drove by on his way to the afternoon shift down the mine. Laurence stopped the car and assisted Grace to her feet.

'Please don't mention this to Paul. I don't want him worrying,' pleaded Grace.

However, her words must have fallen on deaf or mischievous ears, for within an hour, her husband arrived home with an anxious look on his face.

'The whole colliery knows about your tumble. Laurence put it on the Tannoy system for me to go home as soon as possible, to look after you,' he said whilst composing himself. 'I felt sick with worry on hearing the message.'

Paul had rushed home still covered in black coal dust. His eyes rimmed with thick black lines, which almost looked like skilfully applied kohl eyeliner. *He looked rather attractive*, she thought, *almost exotic looking, deep and interesting with the sooty lashes framing his soft brown eyes.*

'No time for a shower I'm afraid. Not when my first child might have a rude awakening from his comfort zone and make an imminent arrival.'

Grace, smiled and joked, 'His arrival? We may well be having a daughter. To be honest, son or daughter, I am just so happy that we are to become parents.'

Paul winked at her. 'So am I,' he smiled.

Grace knew she was fortunate to have Paul. He was a good husband, in fact, one of the best. Whilst she reassured him everything was okay, he insisted on tucking her up on the sofa with a blanket and hot milk.

As she sat sipping her drink, she stared out of the window and recollected the highs and lows of their ten-year marriage. During the last five years, they had been trying for a family, with little luck. Every month, Grace hoped that her body would not betray her, but month after month she had been disappointed. After four years of being unable to conceive, Grace and Paul went to seek medical help. The process was simple for Paul and his sperm count test result appeared within the normal, lower end range. For Grace the numerous blood tests, examinations, and scans revealed that one of her fallopian tubes was not patent, therefore reducing her chance of pregnancy, but not ruling it out.

Time and patience served them well and by her thirty-fifth birthday, they received the long-awaited news of her pregnancy. At first, Grace didn't believe it, because after so many disappointments she had psychologically detached herself from ever having a positive test result. However, when her period was five weeks late and there was a definite fullness in her breasts, she purchased another HCG testing kit from the local chemist. The elderly lady assistant smiled knowingly yet kindly at Grace, as it was well known amongst local residents that Paul and Grace were desperate for a child.

As Grace rested, Paul contacted the midwife and informed her about the fall. She promised to come over and check on Grace after the clinic finished. At half-past two, the midwife knocked on the door. She reassured them that their baby was okay and still seemed comfy inside.

As the days passed, the weather grew more erratic and Grace's belly grew even larger and more uncomfortable. Whilst she and Paul joked about the gender, she had an intuition that she was having a boy. She could sense his strength and presence ever increasing inside her. They had already discussed names, Anne for a girl and Alfie for a boy.

'Alfie,' Grace whispered and he kicked in reply. *Oh yes,* she thought, *my Alfie will come when he is ready.*

Thirteen days after her due date, Grace went to the General Hospital's maternity ward to be induced. She wasn't ecstatic about her baby being medically assisted into the world, she would have preferred a natural onset of labour. However, on the positive side, it would mean no fast car ride in the middle of the night, like some other couples did. Previously, she had been worried about Paul missing the birth or even turning up in a state of panic, wearing his filthy pit clothes, rubber knee pads, and a sooty face.

On the thirteenth eve after her due date, the midwife settled Grace down for the night and discussed the induction process. She would have an enema in the morning, followed by a saline drip containing a drug which would bring on her contractions and the onset of labour. As it turned out; none of this was necessary. Grace experienced the first labour pains at two o'clock on the morning of Alfie's birth. Once he had started the journey there was no stopping him.

Paul had only just managed to gown-up in the delivery room when Alfie's little head appeared. Paul watched in amazement as Grace and Alfie worked together as a team, to give him his long-awaited son. The midwife delivered Alfie's shoulders and he quickly slipped into the world. A world full of love, hope, and promise.

The arrival of Alfie was no different from the infinite number of births before him. Nothing significant happened. The delivery was straightforward with no complications. The midwives documented that the mother and baby were both well and healthy.

Hours after the joyful birth of her son, Grace stared out of the hospital window at the dancing snowflakes outside. Almost at once, as if by magic they returned to water and trickled down the glass, forming tiny streams until they splashed onto the window ledge. She moved her gaze from the window to the bassinette, where Alfie lay. His plump little arms and legs were tightly wrapped in the soft, white, swaddling blanket to help him feel safe and secure in the outside world, away from the warm and limited space of his mother's uterus. His mother's body, his first home. A home he did not want to leave.

CHAPTER TWO

Alfie

Instinct tells me it's time to make the dangerous journey into the world, despite my comfort within the warm nest. I rather enjoyed stretching my arms and kicking my legs against the walls, but now I'm limited by the lack of space. My limbs are curled tight around my body and the swishing sounds are becoming less. These sounds have comforted me along with the strange vibrations echoing around me.

I can no longer wave my arms around and uncurl my fingers or even stretch my legs or kick at the softness surrounding me. The restriction urges me to change position, which is not easy in such a confined space. Turning requires vast energy. An invisible force is directing me to a specific position until my head is pressed against something. I am being squashed and squeezed so much that I have no option other than to push hard and breakthrough. This is exhausting.

I need to rest between the pushing. Then all of a sudden, there is slackness followed by a strange sensation on top of my head. Something hard and cold is stuck to it and I don't like it, so I push and I keep pushing. As I move forward, a tightness grasps me and I am squeezed and pushed. The rope attached is getting tight. I think about going back to my nest, but everything is getting tighter and tighter. I am being pushed forward, along a stream of warm liquid. It's all happening so fast.

Just when I think the journey is over, everything comes to a momentary halt. Then my shoulders are turned sideways and I am abruptly propelled forward. The rope becomes slack. Coolness hits my face and then my body. I don't like it. I want the warmth again. I want my nest.

Something inside me opens and closes, making my chest bigger. A piercing, strange, and high-pitched cry comes from within me. I'm surrounded by strange noises, nothing like the soothing noises in my nest. Something is wrapped around my cold, wet body. It is not soft, wet, and warm such as was surrounding me before. This is tight, heavy, and rough against my skin. I don't like it. Furthermore, the high-pitched cry continues and I can't stop it. Even when I am laid across a warm, soft, almost familiar nest-like place, I still cry. However, when I suckle, a sweet liquid trickles into my mouth and finally the noises within me stop. This is nice, it changes everything.

CHAPTER THREE

Paul looked on proudly as his wife Grace lovingly cradled their newborn son in her arms. They were a vision of health and loveliness. Grace and Alfie appeared content and in that moment, it was as if no one else in the world mattered to either one of them. They were one, as though the umbilical cord had never been cut. He knew for certain it had, for the midwife asked if he wanted to do the honour himself. Paul didn't display the slightest hesitation when asked to perform the significant event of cutting the umbilical cord, which supplied his son with nutrients from the blood of Grace. However, he predicted that the bond between them might never break and an invisible umbilical cord would forever remain. Paul could not take his eyes off them. He gazed at Grace, his eyes filled with the warmth of love and joy.

'It's best if you go home now, so your wife can rest,' the midwife on duty advised Paul.

Alfie's eyes were getting heavy and little sleep sounds escaped from his cute mouth. He gave his wife a gentle hug.

'Shall I bring anything when I return later,' he asked.

Grace reached for her husband's hand and stroked it.

'Thank you, Paul, for giving us such a beautiful baby. The only thing I want is for you to bring yourself. I love you so much and now I have doubled my love. My world is complete.' She leaned towards her husband and kissed him softly on his lips, they lingered for a moment. Paul then left his wife and son in the capable hands of the maternity staff.

CHAPTER FOUR

The porter wheeled Grace and Alfie to the post-delivery ward to join all the other new mothers and babies. A midwife placed Alfie in a Perspex bassinette at the side of his mother's bed. Grace felt exhausted beyond belief. As she drifted off to sleep, she considered the term labour and thought, *yes, it's the right word. Hard labour and a labour of love, but worth every pain and every ounce of energy spent.*

At times the pain became excruciating, but the midwife told her she would forget the pain the moment she held her baby in her arms.

How true. For Grace, the whole experience seemed phenomenal, a long-awaited miracle. Over the next few days in the hospital, Grace and Alfie ate, slept, and cuddled. The midwives informed her about breastfeeding on-demand. They also taught her how to wind and bathe Alfie, as well as change his nappies.

Alfie appeared a very content baby and other than making little mewing sounds, he never cried. This surprised Grace, as she observed that other babies on the ward always cried.

Hospital policy encouraged new mums to stay on the ward for a few days, so the midwives could monitor mother and babies. All of their eager family and friends came to visit them at the hospital, many bringing thoughtful gifts. Grace's parents came first and they brought Alfie an afghan blanket which they had purchased on their recent travels.

Pam, Grace's sister also visited and they spent time catching up on gossip. Various friends, including Paul's work colleagues, popped in to give them well wishes and small gifts. Alfie was given many sleepsuits, cardigans, and matinee jackets including a full layette, which Paul had chosen with a little help from his mother-in-law.

Grace stayed in the maternity ward for five days and for all of this time Alfie was content. However, on day six, this changed.

CHAPTER FIVE

Alfie

I rather got used to the new nest they placed me in after snuggling up to Mother's breast and drinking the warm sweet milk. The thing is, I could see outside of the bassinette, including the shapes and colours around me. I also listened to all of the sounds. My whole body absorbing and feeding off these things, connecting me to life, like the big cord that attached me to Mother. The cord provided safety, it connected me almost like a lifeline. It took some getting used to being without that lifeline, then I discovered that Mother remained close at all times.

I think I prefer to lay on my side, especially when facing Mother. I observe her gaze upon me and I attempt to do something to make her happy. Unfortunately, all I can do is purse my lips and stick out my tongue a little.

I enjoy it when Mother changes my position. Though when I'm on my back, I can only see sparkly lights unless someone leans over the bassinette and pulls faces at me. Father seems to do this rather a lot.

For five days, I tolerated this routine, milk in one end and some awful substance coming out of my other end without giving me a warning. Then everything changed.

After my delightful feed, Mother replaced my soft and fluffy suit with thick, rough, itchy clothes which felt uncomfortable. Even worse, she tried to push my little, fat feet into a tight space. Not nice at all. However, worse horrors were approaching. Instead of being placed into the bassinette which I had grown fond of, Mother placed me in an altogether different nest, with deep, dark sides. A heavy blanket suffocated my body and prevented me from moving my arms and legs. This frightened me and I needed to let Mother know how unhappy I had become. Perhaps if I made the same noise as the other babies on the ward do, then surely, she would lift me out of this horrible nest. At first, I tried a soft noise, but no one paid attention. So, I upped the volume. This time it had an effect.

CHAPTER SIX

Grace lifted Alfie out of the carrycot and gently rocked him in her loving arms. She kissed each tear-stained cheek and whispered, 'I love you, Alfie. I love you with all my heart and I always will.' Her heart filled with such overwhelming love and devotion and a determination to be the best possible mother she could be. However, she was already questioning whether she would be good enough for her darling boy.

'Now, my sweetheart, it is time to leave the hospital. Your father has been working hard to make a nursery for you to sleep and play in.' She cuddled him and then sighed, 'we are going home and I for one am looking forward to sleeping in my own bed, with your father next to me. I haven't slept well here, with all those screaming babies.'

Alfie whimpered and Grace reassured him.

'Don't worry, I will always keep you close by.' She returned Alfie to the carrycot, covering him in the afghan blanket her parents had brought him.

He cried immediately and it got louder and louder. It was a piercing cry that hurt her ears and made her head spin. She began to panic. As Paul made his way towards them, he looked worried.

'Are you alright, Grace? Whatever is wrong with Alfie? His face is scarlet red, he looks very hot.' Paul removed the afghan blanket, but Alfie continued to scream. 'Perhaps he is in pain, what shall we do?' Paul asked.

Grace did not answer at first and when she did, her voice was high-pitched and shaky.

'I'm not sure. He has been fed and winded, his nappy changed. I really don't know. It's the first time this has happened.' She tried hushing Alfie but to no avail. 'I don't know what to do,' she confessed. 'Perhaps I am not going to be any good at this. I feel all stressed and panicky over the smallest thing.'

Paul hugged his wife and took the carrycot from her. 'Perhaps he will be settled when we get home. Come on, let's go to the car.'

As they left the hospital, a fierce wind was blowing outside, so Paul put the hood up on the carrycot and secured the blanket again.

Alfie continued to scream fiercely.

With his free hand, Paul held his wife's tiny trembling hand. 'Come on Grace, let me drive you home.'

CHAPTER SEVEN

Alfie

No matter how hard I cry, nobody lifts me from this horrible nest. Things get worse when Father pulls a dark roof over the cot. The rocking from side to side is horrible, not a gentle movement compared to my Mother's nest. Every time Mother walked, I knew, as it would gently swish and sway me within the surrounding warm water. No, this rocking is not nice. It is harsh and rigid. Not soft and gentle. I hear Mother and Father talking, her voice sounds different, high-pitched and shaky. She sounds as unhappy as me.

Eventually, the movement stops and I am grateful, as all that crying has exhausted me. I am intrigued as to what will come next and I am pleasantly surprised. A relaxing whirring noise and a different, more gentle movement commences. My first car ride and I rather like it.

Mother and Father introduce me to 'my home.' A strange place which smells of flowers. At first, I don't like it and it takes a few weeks to grow fond of it. Mother and Father, keep carrying me from one room to the next, in order to 'get used' to my surroundings. Mother appears delighted to be back at this magical place she calls home. I'm not so sure.

My first home, deep inside Mother's body was the place I felt safe, even though it had become snug.

Father is excited when Mother carries me into a room, he refers to as the nursery. Mother must be excited too, for she lays me down onto a soft squidgy thing and tightly hugs my father.

CHAPTER EIGHT

Paul carried his long-awaited son into their lovingly prepared, cosy home. His ambition of being a good father propelled him to create a safe home for his only child. So, whilst Grace was in the hospital, Paul made the house secure. He even placed a huge brass fireguard around the entire hearth.

The cold weather forced Paul to leave the Charnwood stove on. Upon arriving home, he flicked the damper and within seconds a warm glow appeared. The flames licked up the chimney, creating a cosy atmosphere within the lounge.

As a miner, he received concessionary coal – which was useful. Whilst the coal was messy, the advantages far outweighed the disadvantages. They always had lots of hot water and warm radiators which were fed by the back boiler. Their humble, warm house was snug; perfect for them to raise their son.

Paul placed the carrycot into the stand, which doubled up as a base for the baby bath too. He removed the thick afghan blanket and replaced it with a thin, cream, soft shawl over Alfie.

'Sit down, Grace. Put your feet up and I'll put the kettle on. You look rather exhausted.'

Paul walked into the kitchen and continued to talk. 'It must be the night feeds. This feed on-demand is alright for Alfie, I'm not so sure about you. I dare say you are only getting four hours sleep a night. You can't keep that up for long before it tells on you. Are you certain about breastfeeding? He seems a hungry boy.'

Grace sat down on the velour chair next to the carrycot. She placed a protective hand on the side and gazed at her sleeping, newborn son. Grace was grateful for Paul and knew he meant well, but sheer determination drove her in persisting with breastfeeding. No matter how hard others perceived it; she would persist. The midwives drilled it into mothers that breast was best for baby - anyhow she loved it. She loved snuggling with him and the maternal feelings it gave her when he drew the milk from her body. *The elixir of young life*, thought Grace.

While Paul finished up in the kitchen, Grace became lost in her own thoughts. She wondered how such a small creature could make her so emotional. Her maternal love was consuming and frightening. For with this love came responsibility and with responsibility came anxiety. Grace's anxiety embarrassed her and she had yet to reveal it to Paul. After all, she wasn't a young mother compared to most and had been preparing for motherhood for a long time. *So why was she so anxious?*

By the time Paul came in with tea and biscuits, Grace was sobbing.

'Now then love, what's this all about? We have everything we ever dreamed of,' he said whilst holding her hand. 'Do you think that you may have that baby blues thing? Perhaps we should talk to the health visitor when she calls tomorrow?'

Grace nodded her head, shame swept over her. She didn't want her weakness to affect Paul. The last thing she wanted was for him to worry about her when he was working in such dangerous conditions down the coal mine. To secure additional income, Paul put himself forward to work in a riskier area of the mine. Early in the pregnancy, they had sat down and worked out their finances. They had mutually agreed that due to a lack of free childcare, Grace would need to leave her job.

However, Paul declared that he would like to provide his family with a bigger house. He advised they could achieve this if he took on a higher-paid position working in a dangerous area of the mine.

He also forewarned her that he would secure as much overtime as he could.

Grace paused from her thoughts and sipped the hot, sweet, milky tea. After only two sips, Alfie stirred in his carrycot., his pursed little lips making sucking sounds. At that precise moment, milk leaked through the breast pads and a stain appeared on her cotton blouse. The buttons straining; ready to pop. She unfastened the buttons and lifted Alfie out of his carrycot and placed him on her right breast. As if he had his own homing in device, Alfie latched straight on and eagerly drank her milk. Grace loved his delightful smell, a mix of fragrant baby clothes, milk, and new life.

Paul looked on and smiled as his son hungrily drank nature's food. *Life is so wonderful*, thought Paul. I am the luckiest man in the world.

CHAPTER NINE

Alfie

I enjoy the warm fluid called milk that Mother's body makes especially for me. Just one snag though, sometimes I drink so much, that I almost burst. This causes discomfort in my tummy, followed by a funny taste in my mouth. It makes me cry. So, Mother lifts me up over her shoulder and does a strange tapping movement on my back. This results in a loud funny noise and can cause milk to shoot out of my mouth and dribble down her back. My tummy settles, but I doubt that Mother likes the wet back?

I rather enjoy laying upright on Mother and looking over her shoulder. It makes me the same height, so I can see what she can see. My head wobbles, perhaps my neck is not strong enough or maybe my head is too big and heavy. It makes things difficult, which is why I think Mother lays me back down in the carrycot. I dislike this dark, deep carrycot and crave for the bassinette, so I can look at my surroundings.

Mother and Father love this place they call 'home' and keep telling me how happy I will be here. The thing is, I am only happy when I am close to Mother. As I lay in her warm embrace, I savour the scent of milk and lavender soap. As soon as I am far from her,

I have an uncomfortable disturbance inside. Perhaps it is fear. I'm not sure, but it makes me cry, and once I start, I can't stop until I am so exhausted that I have no energy left to push those tears further down the stream I have created. I know my actions upset Mother and make Father cross. I can hear it in the tone of their voices. Their anger and frustration make me cry even more.

Upon being introduced to the place they proudly call 'home,' they take me to the nursery room. Mother and Father appear excited about this room, they walk around it and point at bright shapes and colours. I am placed in a crib, which is nicer than the carrycot as I can see between the white wooden bars. It's an improvement, but I would rather be in Mother's arms.

Every night, Mother bathes, feeds, and then rocks me in the crib. She sings, song after song in her high-pitched tuneless voice. It hurts my ears, so I pretended to be asleep just to put an end to the painful noise. Mother tiptoes out of the nursery and leaves me alone in the dark room, this scares me and makes me lonely. So, I cry as loud as possible to get Mother back into the nursery, it appears to do the trick. Some nights she sits at the side of the crib and holds my fingers in her hand, we curl and circle our fingers together. I know Mother loves me. I am certain of it, as she must get tired and stiff doing this every night.

As I grow bigger, they replace the crib with a larger version called a cot bed. It has a dangly thing over my head, called a mobile, featuring different colour shapes. It makes a nice musical sound as it moves round and round.

Mother says it's a lullaby and I find it comforting.

Whilst I don't like the cot bed, it is better than the crib. As I grow stronger I develop the ability to roll from one end to the other, this seems to make Mother and Father laugh. I like making them laugh.

Mother is consistent and undertakes the same routine every night: bath, feed, cuddle, and out of tune singing. I find comfort in the routine, as I always know what to expect next. However, my favourite part of the routine is feeding from Mother. I love cuddling up to her. Unfortunately, I no longer have Mother's milk during the day, instead, she gives me an altogether different drink in a bottle. Also, a few times a day she attempts to push squashy food into my mouth. Some of it tastes okay, but not as nice as Mother's milk, which I only drink at bedtime. My night-time routine with Mother feels special and reassuring. However, sometimes friends and family visit, so Mother does not stay long after the feed. I don't like my routine changing, it makes me uneasy, sad, and frightened.

Most days Mother takes me out in a moving cot called a pram. When I'm laying down I don't like it. However, as soon as I am big enough to sit up and look around at all of the interesting sights, I start to rather enjoy it. Mother secures me in using a harness, so I don't fall out and hurt myself.

Whilst I am out in the pram, people stop and chat with Mother. They then lean into me and stroke my cheek with their rough, smelly hands. I hate it. I squirm and move away from their horrid touch, but the harness restricts me. So, I have to endure these violations with distaste and convey a frightened facial expression to get Mother's attention. Why doesn't she understand that I don't like other people touching me? I prefer Mother's touch, she is gentle, comforting, and familiar. Sometimes it takes Mother awhile to figure out what is upsetting me, but she always tries hard to find a solution.

Father is the opposite of Mother and struggles to soothe me. He tries and I know he loves me, but he doesn't understand me. For example, he doesn't seem to realise that his spiky chin tickles my face so much that it overwhelms my senses. I am also irritated by the strong stench of coal, which doesn't seem to disappear even after he has a wash.

His play style is also different to Mother's. He interrupts what I am focusing on and instigates games he thinks we should play; not what interests me. I cry and he becomes cross. So, I cry even louder until it builds up into what Mother calls a 'tantrum.' I spiral out of control, it's almost like being possessed. Multiple emotions and sensations go through my body and I can't use words to express myself. Instead, I kick my arms and legs about and scream until my mouth is all frothy with spit and my face scarlet red.

I enjoy stacking up my wooden bricks and placing my toys in long lines. It's comforting and familiar. The first time I did this Mother clapped and smiled and it made me happy. So, I keep doing it over and over again. Another fascination is the washing machine. I enjoy sitting on the floor watching it spin round and round. It's mesmerising.

One day, I overhear Father tell Mother that it is not normal behaviour and she becomes upset. Mother doesn't like to hear anything bad said against me, even from my own Father. She defends my every action and offers an explanation as to why I am doing it. I believe Mother only sees good in people, including my Father.

Upon learning to stand and walk, or 'finding my feet' as Mother calls it, there is no stopping me. There is so much to see, so many things to explore. Everything is a mystery. As I toddle around my home, I use my senses to touch, smell, listen, and even taste everything around the house. Some discoveries are not nice. For example, fluffy cotton wool toys and shiny plastic can cause a bad reaction within me.

Also, when Mother accidentally scrapes a dinner plate with a knife, it makes a screeching noise and I have to cover my ears and grind my teeth. Whenever this happens, the sensations going through my head are overwhelming.

Some sensations provide comfort, such as snuggling against Mother when she wears her dressing gown. Every morning, before she changes out of her nightwear she lifts me onto her lap and I enjoy snuggling against her comfy dressing gown. As I sit close to Mother, I wrap her long hair around my fingers until it becomes a tight knot, I then let it go until it springs back against her head.

This is our special morning ritual, until one day, Mother replaces the soft dressing gown with a new towelling bathrobe. As she lifts me into her lap, the rough fabric feels horrible against my skin and a wave of unrest passes through me. My whole body goes stiff and my face screws up like a scrunched-up toad. I cry, softly at first and then an uncontrollable squeal. Mother, fortunately, understands what the problem is. She fetches her old dressing gown and wraps it around me until I calm down.

Later in the day, she sews a little blanket out of her old dressing gown and passes it to me. It's wonderful against my skin and it smells of Mother too. Every night I take the blanket with me to bed, holding it makes my body and mind relax.

The health visitor advises Mother to join the local mother and toddler group in order to get 'out and about.' As soon as we arrive, it is obvious that I am different to the other children, or rather my behaviour is.

Nobody wants to play with me and I don't really want to play with them. Mother seems to be happy to talk to the other women, but I really hate it. I do like the ride-on car they have though, and I feel compelled to keep riding it. This annoys the other children and makes their angry mothers shake their heads, wag their fingers, and even shout at me. This continues until a scary looking woman takes it away from me. I don't understand why? I am only playing pretend games like the others and I enjoy pretending to crash into their tricycles.

Week after week, Mother perseveres and withstands spiteful looks and unkind words thrown in her direction. I don't understand the rules of play. So instead, I sit alone in a corner stacking and lining up the wooden bricks in straight lines. This activity comforts me, even though Mother no longer claps when I do it. Instead, she looks upset and almost embarrassed. One week we don't go and that is the end of that.

CHAPTER TEN

P aul, I'm confused. Alfie is such a gorgeous little boy. Full of love and affection with me, yet others don't seem to understand him,' said Grace, as they sat drinking coffee.

'At times, he appears locked in his own little world. He attempts to connect with other children, but doesn't succeed. Nobody else appears to understand him, or even have patience with him and that includes you too. Why?' she asked her husband.

Paul sighed. He felt exhausted and in no mood to talk about Alfie. Every single bloody night was the same. Alfie wakes up screaming, Grace jumps out of bed and takes a while to soothe him. Why couldn't that boy sleep through the night like *normal* kids?

He turned to Grace and replied, 'Come on love, surely you realise that Alfie is not like other boys?'

She looked defensive, but he continued.

'Alfie's an intense, high-maintenance kid and he looks like he's on another planet sometimes. No matter how hard I try, I can't get him to enjoy the usual boyish games. Instead, he spends hours stacking and lining things up, or watching the washing machine. It's not normal.'

Grace didn't reply. She pursed her lips and thought about what he had said.

Paul used the opportunity to scrutinise his wife. He realised that he no longer recognised the beautiful woman he fell in love with all those years ago. Back then she was stunning. Petite with luscious, long, dark hair, and pretty, almond-shaped, brown-eyes.

Today, Grace was a shadow of her former self. Thin, long, lank hair framed her gaunt, tired face. Her puffy eyes had dark circles underneath. She doesn't even apply make-up or style her hair any-more he noted. Grace was so consumed with Alfie, she neglected her appearance. Paul wondered, if he could get Alfie sorted, then perhaps his wife would get better.

'Grace, I think you need to talk to the health visitor about our concerns. I'm on the afternoon shift next week, book an appoint-ment and we can go together.'

As requested, Grace organised an appointment. However, the health visitor appeared more interested in Alfie's height, weight, and vaccination status than his emotional and behavioural devel-opment.

'Your lad is growing nice and tall. He is on the highest centile,' said the health visitor and she showed them the growth chart.

'But what about his peculiar ways?' asked Grace.

'Nothing to worry about. Every child develops at their own pace,' the health visitor reassured her.

Paul thought otherwise, but the health visitor's conclusion gave his wife a temporary lift and made her anxious face lighten up. He could see that Alfie was different and wondered whether it was nature or nurture. Perhaps Grace's parenting style was reinforcing it. She was far too gentle and always rushing to solve his problems.

'Grace, you need to be firm and not give in to his tantrums,' he chided her. 'Alfie is running circles around you.' Paul believed their son needed discipline, after all, his parents were strict and he turned out okay.

Grace didn't agree with spanking and wondered if Paul grasped the concept of respectful parenting. He obviously didn't consider that his proposed methods may make Alfie worse. Paul constantly criticised her and evidently didn't appreciate everything she did for the family. Their marriage was becoming strained and she knew they were drifting apart. On the rare occasions he was home and they spoke, he appeared bored. Her only conversational topic was Alfie.

'Anything new to tell me?' Paul asked as soon as she talked about her day.

But what could she talk about? Housework, cooking, cleaning, and childcare was the extent of her life these days. She had little time to pursue any hobbies, like the keep-fit classes some of the younger mothers went to. Grace was becoming more isolated, especially since she stopped going to the mother and toddler group.

Her parents were travelling again and her sister worked full-time. Even if she made new friends, what would she even talk about? She had no time or interest to follow the latest pop stars or TV soaps and she no longer had time to read novels. Grace only knew Alfie and had little else to talk about. Motherhood had consumed her and it was affecting her relationship with Paul. She guessed that her husband disapproved of her everyday uniform of baggy jeans and practical tops. Grace knew she was not alluring like those Charlie's Angels, Paul drooled over on TV.

Once he said, 'Grace, look at these American ladies. Ain't they glamorous!'

It knocked her confidence. Their love life was almost non-existent due to sheer exhaustion and a lack of interest. She wished that she could get dressed up in her finery and show Paul that she was still desirable. However, even an evening at the Miners Welfare Club proved impossible. She didn't really trust anyone to care for her precious Alfie. She doubted that they would care for him like she does. Anyhow, it would disturb his routine and cause a meltdown.

Paul loved socialising and continued to enjoy a well-earned pint or two at the Welfare Club with his mates. They played cards, talked football and recently politics. Home life had become boring for Paul and he needed to escape Grace's martyrdom. In a desperation to avoid home, he took Alfie to the playground where he smoked and chatted with some of the young mothers.

Every Sunday he met his father for a pint and a game of dominoes, whilst Grace stayed at home preparing a traditional Sunday dinner with the full trimmings.

Once, she said, 'Paul, how about we take Alfie with us for a drive into the countryside and a pub lunch?'

'Don't be daft,' he replied. 'A pub lunch in the countryside would cost an arm and a leg.'

It was frustrating how he religiously kept up the Sunday pint and home-cooked dinner ritual. Most local men were the same, they all considered it their basic right and the women had to accept it. She contemplated arguing with Paul about women's rights, but she didn't have the energy and most likely it would fall on deaf ears.

Grace felt invisible, to her husband and the rest of the world. Only Alfie saw and needed her. Her parents were off gallivanting around the world.

'Spending the family inheritance,' she joked last time she saw them. Grace too craved sun, sand, and sangria. She longed to take Alfie to the seaside, but money was tight. She envied her parents and loathed the freedom they enjoyed - didn't they realise she was struggling? Though to be fair, she hadn't talked to her parents about her situation. They presumed Grace and Paul had a happy marriage and were delighted that their dream of having a child came true. Her hardworking parents were enjoying the labours of their life.

'It's our time to have fun,' they told their daughters. 'So, we are selling up and living life to the full.'

They cashed in their pensions, auctioned family heirlooms, and sold their lovely family home. When not travelling, they stayed in a tiny rented flat. Grace predicted that they would soon spend all their money and end up on benefits, claiming to 'be needy elderly dependents.' This disgusted her.

Grace had never been political, but wanted to become better informed so tuned into BBC Radio 4 whilst she ironed. A recent broadcast inferred that the current political situation was 'volatile' and industrial strikes may start occurring up and down the country. Paul expressed his concern to Grace about unrest in the mining industry.

'It won't be long till Arthur Scargill rallies enough support from the miners to call for industrial action,' he informed her.

This scared Grace, as they relied upon the mining industry for their sole income.

Vast, contrasting thoughts stacked up inside of her mind, tumbling around and tangling up like washing in the tumble dryer.

'My mind is spinning,' she told Alfie one day when she was too tired to play with him.

This made him cry. 'Alfie, my precious. I'm alright sweetie. Just give me five minutes.'

Grace was conflicted. She loved to play with Alfie, but sometimes craved alone time. She was surprised, yet grateful when Paul started taking Alfie to the swimming pool and playground.

However, when they returned Paul always complained, 'That lad ain't right!'

Grace was unsure what happened on their outings, but Alfie always appeared subdued and deep in thought afterwards.

Grace wanted Alfie to have a magical childhood. So, during the hot summer days, she spent hours playing with him in the garden. One day, as he was playing with diggers in the sandpit, she realised how tall and handsome he had become. Earlier that day, she received a letter confirming his nursery school placement and felt apprehensive. How would he cope at nursery without her?

CHAPTER ELEVEN

Alfie

Mother tells me that her head is spinning, but it's not, it's sitting perfectly still on her neck. I'm confused and even more so when she tells me to give her five minutes. How can I give her time? I want to make Mother happy, but I don't know how.

I enjoy being with Mother. I follow her around the house and observe all her strange activities. Sometimes she moves a hot steamy object all over our clothes, she calls this ironing. I'm not allowed to touch it, but I love the sound it makes. However, it can be difficult to hear over the strange voices coming from the box called a radio.

Mother tells me that 'Father is working hard down the mines to put bread and butter on the table.'

I don't see him often, but when he comes home Father takes me to the playground. He encourages me to play with the other children. He thinks I don't see, but I see everything, much more than he realises. Whilst I'm playing he chats and talks to the mothers at the playground.

He asks them 'if they want a fag?' Father passes them foul-smelling smoking sticks, which they place in their red stained lips.

He laughs and jokes with these mothers and talks about TV programmes. He doesn't laugh much with Mother.

I don't play with the other children at the playground. They keep running around screaming aimlessly, climbing up the metal frames and swinging on the metal handles. Sometimes they fall and their mothers come running over to soothe them. Surprisingly, it works, for they are soon running around again. I prefer to sit in one of the tunnels and line the stones up on the floor that I have collected and stored in my trouser pockets.

Actually, I think it suits Father quite well, that he doesn't need to look out for me. He knows where I am and I can't get hurt, but what he doesn't know, is that I creep to the end of the tunnel and watch him.

There is one mother, who is always at the playground at the same time as us. Father stands very close to her and they smoke the foul-smelling 'fag' sticks together. They laugh and sometimes they hold hands when he thinks no one can see. However, I see everything and I remember too.

At times like this, I close my eyes and think of Mother. I picture her kind eyes and it makes me feel better. Whilst I'm thinking about this, Father repeatedly shouts my name and gets annoyed when I don't respond straight away.

'Come on,' he yells. 'Let's go home for tea.'

Upon arriving home, Father always puts the TV on for me and then takes Mother into the kitchen as he thinks I can't hear.

Father says to Mother, 'That lad ain't right Grace. He should be running around playing football like the others. You are turning him into a mummy's boy, always attached to your bloody apron strings.'

I hear Mother defending me and her voice sounds all high-pitched and shaky. I think she is upset.

After tea, Father says 'I'm off to the club to play cards' and he goes out again. I don't understand why he doesn't play at home.

When Father is out, Mother is more relaxed and plays in a way that makes me happy.

'What adventures shall we have Alfie?' she asks. So, I grab the train set and I make a long, beautifully straight line across the floor. Mother knows that the curvy tracks make me feel funny, so she got rid of them all. I like pushing and pulling the train back and forth along the perfectly straight track. It feels good, it makes me happy.

I think trains are fascinating, even those on TV like Thomas the Tank Engine. Mother knows this, so when they swap the cot for a big boy bed, she buys me Thomas the Tank Engine bedsheets and matching curtains. I really like my room now and my new bed is lovely as it's big enough for Mother to lay down next to me when I'm upset. Sometimes she falls asleep before me and when I wake up in the morning she is still there holding on to me, as though afraid that I might disappear.

When the weather gets warmer, Father says it's time I learnt to swim and develop some muscles. On his days off, he takes me to the local children's pool. It smells. There is an overpowering scent, which Father tells me is chlorine. It overloads my senses, but I'm not afraid of the water. In fact, I rather enjoy splashing about in the pool. I stay away from the other children, as I don't understand the rules of the games they play. They shout and scream, their shrill voices echoing around the large room. This becomes overwhelming, so I walk along the side of the pool and touch the edges. It gives me an instant relief. Father doesn't like me doing this and pushes me towards the other children.

'Go and play with the kids,' he urges me.

I look at them and know they don't want to play with me and I don't want to play with them.

The smelly 'fag' lady from the playground is always at the swimming pool too. Her sons are older, bigger, and fatter than me. Nevertheless, Father always encourages me to go away and play with them so that he can chat with their mother, who is half naked in the pool.

'Looking good,' he says to her as she poses at the side of the pool.

I don't think she looks good. She has an orange face and blood red lips. Her hair is big, yellow, and stiff. Father always stays close to her, they laugh and talk about silly things.

When Father is at work, Mother takes me to the pool and I really enjoy it. Fortunately, we never see the orange faced smelly lady. She only seems to be there when I'm with Father. Strange.

Mother is great fun. She pretends to be a shark and chases me in the water; it makes me laugh. She also tells me to stand on the side of the pool and as she moves further from the edge, encourages me to jump in. I trust Mother and I know I am safe, so I do as she asks. Mother always treats us to hot chocolate and biscuits in the café afterwards. Yummy.

One hot summer day, as Mother and I play in the garden, she says, 'Oh Alfie, it will be strange when you are not next to me all day.'

I stop playing with the digger in the sandpit lining and turn around to listen to her.

'You see Alfie,' she continues. 'You are a big boy now, so will be starting nursery in September.'

I am confused. I thought my bedroom was the nursery?

'I am going to buy you some new, big boy clothes,' she says happily.

So, we go on the bus to the town centre. During the bus ride, Mother sings my favourite song, 'The wheels on the bus go round and round.'

We quickly do the shopping and then she declares that I needed a 'professional' haircut, instead of the bowl cut she usually gives me.

This frightens me; I don't like strangers touching me. Mother takes me to the hairdressers which specialise in children's haircuts. They have cartoons on and it relaxes me. Whilst we are waiting, I catch a glimpse of the orange faced, smelly fag lady Father talks to. I don't say anything to Mother.

When the 'special day' arrives, Mother dresses me up and then proudly walks me to the nursery. I feel anxious, so I trail my hand along the buildings and it makes me feel better.

As we approach a grey, square-shaped building, Mother announces 'here is your nursery school.' She rummages in her bag and pulls out the camera.

'Excuse me, please can you take a photo of my son and I together?' she asks another mother. As I stand outside the square-shaped building, I try to look cute as Mother calls it and I smile my biggest smile when the kind lady asks me to.

When we get to the door leading into the school, I notice that some of the little girls are crying and clinging to their mother's. I am not afraid to go to this new place. I will find a quiet corner and amuse myself. I am shown to a little peg with a picture of a green dinosaur above it.

'This is your coat peg, Alfie,' says Mother. 'Now be a very good boy for your teacher, Miss Sharrow, she will look after you until I return.' A quick hug and kiss and Mother is gone, waving to me as she leaves.

I follow the children into the classroom and sit down cross-legged on the floor with the other children facing Miss Sharrow. I find it hard to sit still without fidgeting, so I rock myself back and forth on the floor while Miss Sharrow reads us a story.

As promised, Mother comes to collect me, all the while asking me questions about my time at school. What is there to say? I sat with the other children for story time, but for the rest of the morning, I was happy to play on my own, putting the little cars in a row.

CHAPTER TWELVE

Whilst Alfie was at nursery school, Grace got two hours every morning to theoretically catch up on housework. However, the four walks backwards and forwards to the school every day exhausted her. After she returned home, she cleared away the breakfast dishes, tidied around the house, and then it was time to set off again.

When Paul was on the afternoon shift, he went in early to attend the increasing number of meetings being held about the upset within the mining industry, meaning he wasn't around to take some of the strain from his wife. Paul knew that Grace was not looking well. She had lost a lot of weight since Alfie was born and just didn't seem like the woman he married. She had lost interest in her appearance, and in any form of physical activity in the marital bed, claiming that she was always too tired.

He knew how much of herself she gave to Alfie, trying to be the perfect mother, but what about being the perfect wife? Had that slipped her mind? She had breastfed Alfie way beyond what he considered acceptable. Played with him for most of the day and stayed with him in his bedroom for most of the night. Alfie still wasn't sleeping through the night and so she didn't disturb Paul when he had an early start on the day shift, she spent many a night in there in case Alfie needed her.

For months, he encouraged her to visit the doctor's surgery to discuss her declining health, without much response. In the end, he booked an appointment for her.

At first, Grace was not happy that Paul had taken it upon himself to arrange the appointment and now here she was, sat in front of a very austere looking doctor who was saying something to her about her blood test results.

'I don't understand, Dr Freeman. What do you mean I have pernicious anaemia?' she asked anxiously. 'What exactly does that mean? Can I make it go away if I eat the right foods with lots of iron? I've heard that drinking a pint of Guinness a day can help with anaemia; do you think I should give it a try?'

Dr Freeman was shaking his head. 'No, Grace, that won't make any difference. This is not iron deficiency anaemia, although some of the symptoms are similar, particularly the extreme tiredness. This is a deficiency of Vitamin B12.'

'Then I will take some vitamin supplements and eat lots of vitamin B foods,' answered Grace. Dr Freeman was looking at his watch and getting impatient.

'Grace, I'm afraid that is not possible. Your body cannot absorb vitamin B12 from food or tablets. We need to give you an injection, every three months. However, first, we need to give you a booster dose by injection every other day until you have had six and then you may begin to feel a little better.'

That was six appointments to be made, thought Grace. How am I going to fit them all in around Alfie?

As it turned out, she needn't have worried. The kind receptionist arranged all of the appointments to be given in the late afternoon, giving Grace the time to collect Alfie from nursery school and give him lunch before they set off for the surgery.

Although Grace could drive, Paul needed the car for work every day. Since he had been attending the National Union of Mineworkers meetings, of which there seemed to be many, Grace very rarely had the use of the family car, much to her annoyance.

Alfie enjoyed the visits to the surgery and was strangely well behaved. He appeared fascinated by the surroundings and watched with great interest when Grace was given the injection in her upper arm. It was painful, like a sharp bee sting, the nurse had warned her of this. Something to do with the acidity of the red liquid that was being pushed into her muscle. However, as the days went by, Grace was beginning to feel the beneficial effects of the B12 injections.

Truth be told, it wasn't until she began to feel better, that she realised just how unwell she had been.

The walk to the nursery school was becoming less of an effort and she even gained the strength to walk to the new Co-op supermarket instead of the local corner shop. As she shopped for fresh groceries, she also chatted with the shop assistants. They were all local women and their job-roles in the supermarket provided them the opportunity to hear the village gossip.

One of them appeared to know her Paul quite well and asked after him. She said that her name was Hazel. Her husband Stewart, worked with Paul on the same shift. He occasionally joined Paul at the Welfare Club for a pint, adding quite clearly that it was only on occasion, as her husband was not much of a drinker.

Hazel always sought Grace out when she called into the shop. She spoke kindly to her and encouraged Grace to join the local Women's Institute.

'Women needed to support one another, as times were getting difficult,' Hazel said.

Grace felt that Hazel was holding back on something that she wanted to share, but was too kind to say anything disrespectful to her. She considered the possibility that Hazel had noticed, or even heard, gossip about how Alfie was a difficult child to raise.

As the weeks went by, Grace began to feel physically and mentally stronger. She decided to practice self-care and when Alfie was asleep at night time she would watch TV. She was able to choose exactly what she wanted to watch, as Paul was always out.

One evening as she watched the BBC news, there was an announcement that the National Union of Mineworkers was taking industrial action. The news presenter informed viewers, that the miners at Brampton Bierlow, South Yorkshire had walked out. Some expert came on TV stating that up to 20,000 mining jobs needed to be cut. Grace wondered why Paul hadn't told her this. As she sat alone listening to the doom and gloom of the news, she began to think about the state of her marriage. When Paul finally arrived home with the smell of beer on his breath and cigarette smoke on his clothes, Grace realised how much her husband had changed.

'Any more beer left?' Paul asked as soon as he sat down.

Grace was fuming, she turned to him and said, 'You already smell like a brewery.'

Paul looked shocked. He wasn't used to Grace talking like this. 'Fine, I will get myself one,' he slurred and went to the kitchen for a can of Mansfield bitter.

When he sat down, Paul signed heavily. 'You heard the news?' He asked.

Grace nodded and said, 'Will you be going on strike?'

Paul gulped his beer and then began to update Grace on what was happening. He told her that the Nottinghamshire NUM supported strike action, but some members wanted to continue working as they didn't agree with it. Paul explained that he didn't know what to do. His whole family worked or had worked, in the mines of Nottinghamshire. His great-grandfather had helped to sink the first mine in their district and his own father had carried on the family tradition of working the coal face. He felt loyal to his family and fellow miners and didn't want to be a 'scab'. But, if he went on strike, then money would be tight.

'If you go on strike, I will support and stand by you, Paul. However, things will have to change. For starters, you can't spend our money on alcohol and cigarettes. Our budget will be very tight that's for certain.

'Fortunately, I know how to prepare nutritious meals which won't cost much. I think we should grow more vegetables in the garden. Perhaps potatoes, cabbages, and carrots. You should start doing this straight away,' she said to Paul in an unusually assertive voice.

Paul was shocked beyond belief. Grace sounded more like her old self. *Pity, she still looked a total mess*, he thought.

Paul went on strike and initially tried to be constructive with his time. As instructed by Grace, he planted some vegetables and chopped down an old tree at the bottom of their garden for firewood. Unfortunately, along with the loss of wages the concessionary coal stopped too. Their last load of coal would have to be used very carefully.

Paul soon grew bored at home, so began to take Alfie to the local playground every day. Grace thought that this was lovely and hoped it would help them to develop their relationship. However, she noted that Alfie never seemed happy upon their return. She tried to talk to both Paul and Alfie about this, but neither one of them wanted to discuss it.

'Everything's fine Grace, stop fussing,' Paul replied.

However, when Grace looked into her son's eyes, she knew there was something worrying him. He looked like a boy with a secret to tell, he looked conflicted. Grace hated seeing him looking sad and wanted to get to the bottom of it.

As expected money was very tight, so throughout the strike the wives rallied round and supported each other. Whilst Paul took Alfie out, Grace met her friend Hazel and they would talk about the strike.

Hazel informed her that the Women's Institute was helping struggling families. She inquired if Grace would like to help set up a local soup kitchen with funding from the Women's Institute. Grace thought that this was a fantastic idea and threw herself into this new role of helping others. She began to feel empowered by her actions and her confidence soared.

Whilst Grace worked in the soup kitchens, Paul seemed happy to take Alfie out every day. She thought that for a man who was not making any money, he seemed rather jovial at the prospect of going out. Furthermore, she was frustrated that after his evening meal, he would go to the Miner's Welfare Club to get an update about the strike from his mates. Whilst he promised not to drink, he always did, claiming that he didn't spend much.

Grace was angry about this and confided in Hazel, who sympathised. As usual, Grace felt that Hazel wanted to tell her something, but couldn't quite say it out loud. Grace was feeling paranoid. She wondered if the village was gossiping again about how Alfie is different, or questioning her parenting skills. She knew that something was not right.

One day, Grace and Hazel had to close the soup kitchen early due to not having any supplies. So, Grace decided to go to the playground to surprise Alfie and Paul. As she got closer to the playground Grace saw Paul laughing with a heavily made-up young woman. As Grace approached them from behind, she saw Paul lean into the woman to kiss her.

Grace stopped and held her chest. She couldn't breathe, her head began to spin, and anger filled up inside of her. She could forgive Paul for the money he spent on booze and cigarettes, but his betrayal with another woman was too much. Grace found an inner strength and with her head held high, went over to get Alfie from the sandpit.

'Come on sweetheart, you are coming home with me.'

Paul suddenly realised that Grace was there and ran over to them.

'Paul, I will talk to you later,' she calmly called out to him, displaying no evidence of the pain and torment that was surging through her mind. After Alfie was fast asleep, Grace found the courage to confront Paul.

'How could you do this to me and Alfie?'

Paul went red and said, 'It's not what it looks like.'

'Liar,' Grace growled. 'I want you to pack your bags and go, I don't want to even look at you.'

That night Paul slept on the sofa and left upon waking. Grace knew that she had to be a lioness for her Alfie. Paul's indiscretion was not going to ruin his young life. She would find a way of coping without her husband, other women had managed it and so would she, even during such troubled times.

After Paul left, Grace constantly had thoughts whirling around her head and she struggled to sleep. Over and over again she questioned herself as to how she had not seen this coming. Or had she chosen to ignore the warning signs? Surely, she hadn't been so blind? The more Grace turned these thoughts over in her mind, the more confused she became. Each thought perpetuated another, then another until her mind felt overloaded with thoughts.

She complained about it to her friend Hazel, who advised 'Why don't you keep a diary? I write in my diary every week and it really helps me to keep sane. I think about my diary as a friend who I can confide in when times get tough. Sometimes when I reflect on what I have written, it somehow appears less important and certainly nothing to lose sleep over.'

Grace thought about Hazel's wisdom and purchased herself a beautiful leather-bound diary. Whenever Grace felt sad or low, she transferred her thoughts and emotions onto paper, she found it therapeutic and empowering. Although she was a single mother, she was determined to heal and become a strong, independent mother. Someone that Alfie could look up to. A mother he would be proud of.

CHAPTER THIRTEEN

Alfie

For some reason, Father stopped coming home, which, for a while, seemed to upset Mother greatly. She thought I didn't notice her crying, but I heard her most nights in bed, sobbing into the pillow. Most evenings after supper, she sat on the sofa with her legs curled underneath her bottom, writing in a special book called a diary. She always looked deep in thought as she wrote in this special book.

Once, I enquired if she was writing a story. Mother told me that it was a story of sorts, but it was more like me writing in my news book at school. She tried to pretend that she was fine and put on a great act, painting a smile on her face for my benefit. But I see people, especially the falseness - it is as clear as the difference between black and white. To me, there is no grey.

Because Mother was sad, I tried to be a good boy. I tried very hard to sleep at night, but although my arms and legs were tired, my head never was. My mind did not want to sleep. I thought about everything that had happened during the day. In fact, my mind went further back than the day. I also turned over and over in my mind, the things that happened weeks before. I thought ahead, made plans and visualised all kinds of things. Sometimes, frightening thoughts flashed through my mind. My imagination was crazy most of the time, but at night it went into overdrive.

Shortly after I noticed the absence of my Father, there was a number of visitors to the house. Hazel, a friend of Mother's began to call in after she had finished work. She sat at our kitchen table drinking tea and whispering about local gossip. I think it helped a little, she seemed to be the only one to put a smile on Mother's face. Also, my Aunty Pam, who very rarely visited before began to visit more frequently. Sometimes she stayed the night, which I didn't like very much, as it changed Mother's routine with me, making me feel more unsettled at night than usual. My bath time ritual and usual supper of warm milk and biscuits, followed by story time with Mother was disrupted.

I was told, that I was to be nice to Aunty Pam because her husband had recently passed away. I wasn't sure what was meant by that. Where had he passed to? But it must have been something really bad because Aunty Pam cried a lot.

Worse than the crying was the smoking. She smoked one cigarette after the other, making a dirty pile of ash in an old saucer that Mother had provided her with. Our house always smelled funny when she was around, sort of nasty and dirty. I hated the smell which almost felt like my nose was burning inside. At times, the room was so smoky that it made my eyes sting and Mother had to open the windows.

Sometimes I heard both Mother and Aunty Pam, crying together. I guess they didn't realise how thin the walls of our home were, either that, or they were not aware of how acute my young hearing was.

Although Grandmother and Grandfather hadn't visited much in the past, they also began to call around on the weekends when I was not at school. I didn't like my Mother's family very much, they are not like Mother at all. Mother is soft and kind, fluffy around the edges. She smells of fresh grass, sunshine, and flowers. They were sharp, hard, and pointy. Their clothes smelled funny, as though they had been stored in an old, damp, smelly cupboard. Grandma smelled of cabbage and onions; Grandfather of stale tobacco. Usually, when they visited they spoke of Father as though he had done something terribly wrong.

I once heard Grandfather say that Mother had given up on him too easily and should have fought for him. I can never imagine Mother fighting anyone, let alone Father. Grown-ups talk in such funny ways.

Grandma seemed to disagree; she said that Mother was better off without him. 'If he wasn't willing to support his wife looking after their son, just because he wasn't right in the head?'

I guess they were talking about me, but there is nothing wrong with my head. It looks the same as everyone else's except smaller than the grown-ups.

After a while, the visits from Aunty Pam and my grandparents became less and once more. Mother and I began to settle back into a routine that suited me. We had set times for everything and Mother tried to stick to this routine. She knew how upset I became if the day didn't go to plan.

One day she told me, I was to start the big school. All schools looked big to me, so I thought that maybe this new place would be the same as my nursery school. The big school was close to the nursery school. So, on the first day, we set off as usual. However, Mother left me with a different teacher this time. Her name was Miss Tatham. I was very sad not to see Miss Sharrow as I had grown quite fond of her. From somewhere inside of me a funny feeling rose-up. Mother later said it was a tantrum and that she was most embarrassed in front of the other mothers. The funny feeling didn't change anything. Miss Sharrow didn't come, so I was left with Miss Tatham.

There were lots of children in the classroom. Some I recognised from the nursery, others I didn't know at all. One boy, whose name was Philip, came over to me and gave me his toy red car. He grinned at me with his toothy smile. I decided I liked Philip, he could be my best friend.

One day at playtime, some boys came over to me and Philip and they pushed him over for no reason. This made me very angry. So, I thumped both the boys very hard in their faces, just like I have seen on the television, when superheroes defend good people against the villains. I even made blood come from their noses. The teacher blew a loud whistle and came over to me. She lifted me off the floor with my collar, it was very uncomfortable, so I began to cry. Other teachers ran across to the two boys and took them away.

My friend, Philip, just lay there and gawped at the whole scene. No one seemed to care that he had been pushed to the floor and was crying, even though they could see him trying to scramble up. The teacher dragged me from the playground and took me into my classroom, where she made me stand on a chair with my back to the class, for the remainder of the day.

Even when I put my hand up to ask if I may go the toilet, I was ignored and left until my tummy hurt and I could no longer hold myself. A stream of hot wee ran down my legs, making a pool on the chair and the floor. Yet still, the teacher made me stand there. I wanted to cry, but I never did, for I did not want to upset Philip, who was my friend.

When Mother came to collect me from school, she was horrified at my wet trousers and socks. She saw that my legs were sore from the chaffing of the cloth. I handed her a letter the teacher had given me before I left. Mother gave me a hug. She knew how to make me feel better. When we got home, Mother put me in the bath and let me play with the boats. I heard her speaking to someone on the telephone, she sounded very angry.

After Mother had helped me to dry, she rubbed some soft cream on my bottom and my legs. It felt nice. Although early, she dressed me in some soft, clean pyjamas and gave me my little tartan dressing gown to wear.

We sat together on the sofa, watching cartoons. My favourite at the moment is He-Man, although I also like Transformers. They are clever because they disguise themselves as something else. I wish I could transform into something else, maybe into what Grandmother calls a *normal little boy*. I want to be like all the other boys and girls. They all seem to have lots of friends. I wonder if Father did leave Mother because of me?

While we were on the sofa, Mother gently asked me to explain if anything had happened at school to upset me. I told her that I have a friend. That made Mother smile, a big happy smile. I told her what those naughty boys did to Philip and what I did back to them because they hurt my friend.

At first, she didn't say anything. Then Mother asked if Philip had wanted me to help him by hitting the boys. I told her, it was not his fault and that I decided to hit them all by myself.

She told me that I was being a good friend looking out for Philip, but perhaps violence was not the answer. I didn't understand. The two boys had been violent to my friend and they were not in trouble, yet I was. Mother told me that the letter I gave her, was from the teacher, who wanted to see her after school the next day. I didn't want to go to school the next day, but I did want to see my friend. So, I was a brave boy like Mother ask me to be.

Every morning before class we have an assembly. That means all of the children and teachers gather together in a big room called a hall. The teachers talk and we sing songs. I like singing songs, they have a pattern to them called a chorus. I like patterns and shapes. I see other things in the patterns which are hidden away from other people.

That morning, instead of sitting with my classmates like I usually did, a teacher placed me on the stage next to where all the teachers sat. I was a little surprised and very frightened to be standing up there on the big stage, looking down at the children.

Miss Tatham told me to stand straight and still and to put one finger against my closed lips. Then she spoke to all the children and told them what a very naughty boy I had been, for hitting the two boys yesterday and making their nose bleed. She said their parents had put in a complaint and that I was to be punished. No mention was made of punishment to the other boys for pushing Philip first. It all felt very unfair. I realised there and then at such a young age, that life is sometimes unfair and some children are treated differently to others. I knew that I was going to be one of them because I was not like the others.

I did not look anyone in the eyes after this, for I thought it a waste of time. The eyes can lie and mislead. They may appear kind, but behind the false smile and twinkling eyes can lay a falseness, fakery and lies.

At the end of the assembly, I was allowed off the stage to join my class as they left the hall. I caught up with Philip, he smiled at me and held my hand. I knew there and then that I could trust Philip and that he would always be my friend.

I never told Mother about the fear that I felt when the teacher stood me in front of the whole school to be humiliated, but I would remember that feeling and vowed to myself that never again would I be afraid of such circumstances. I would use that experience to my advantage. The fact that I was punished for defending a friend did not change who I was and how I felt. I knew that I would do it again if I felt that it was necessary. Next time I would be more cunning.

After school that day, Mother went to see the headmistress as the letter instructed. She insisted that I was allowed to stay in the room. I think this was not in the rulebook, but my Mother was not about to let anyone walk over her when it came to me and my happiness. She was like a lioness protecting her cub.

Miss Tatham was also present. She told Mother that she had been a teacher for many years and was very experienced and in her opinion, there was something not quite right about me. She said I appeared intelligent as I could memorise whole chunks of verse and stories, even quoting them verbatim, whatever that meant. I don't think Mother understood that either, but she seemed pleased that I had been described as intelligent.

'The problem lays with his personality and behaviour,' she went on to say.

It appears that Miss Tatham had been watching me closer than I thought. She told Mother that I look at her expressionless, just blinking occasionally, it is as though there is no connection, she said.

Then she described something called tics. Not sure what she meant by that, but she started pulling funny faces and moving her shoulders up and down and stretching out her neck. She looked rather funny and I don't know how Mother kept a straight face.

The headmistress interrupted by saying that she highly recommended that I was assessed by a child psychologist as soon as Mother could arrange it.

'You call yourselves teachers and claim to understand the needs of children,' said my Mother. 'Well from my observations you don't appear to have any idea how to fairly treat my son. Not all children are textbook perfect you know. Some children like my Alfie are sensitive in ways that others aren't. He saw an injustice to his friend and acted on it, in the only way he thought possible. He was not being naughty.'

We left that room together, Mother with her head held high and me copying her. The two boys who had pushed over my friend, were outside the door with their parents. Probably there to see if justice had been done.

One of the mothers shouted something at us. Immediately my lioness Mother retaliated in a very controlled voice, using clever words that hit like knives. They soon shut up, as they were cleverly reminded by my Mother, that their two boys were no angels and that their behaviour that day had been the catalyst and she would never forget. The expression on their mean looking faces was a sight I will treasure forever.

I am so proud of Mother; she is not like the others. My Mother doesn't stand at the school gate gossiping and criticising. She doesn't look like all of the other women with their funny clothes. Sometimes, when I see them gathered outside of the school gates, with their hands clasped together, they look just like the local Mafiosi.

I recall the occasion when a young traveller girl spent a term at our school. When her father came to collect her, the other mothers stood well away from him with their pointy noses cocked in the air. They ignored him as if he didn't exist. They probably wouldn't have given him the time of day if he had asked. The little girl, Selina, was sat next to me in class. Although shy, she did chat to me and didn't seem to notice that I was not quite like the other boys. She didn't pass comment about me, rocking backwards and forwards on the chair. I think her reading and writing skills embarrassed her, so I tried to help as much as possible. I think she liked me a little.

I talked to Mother about Selina and she made a special effort to speak to her father when he was waiting outside the school gates, much to the shock and horror of the other parents. I think Mother rather enjoys the fact that she is more open-minded than the others.

She calls them bigots; whatever that means. With time, things settled down at school. I had no problems with the tasks they set. It was all rather easy for me and usually, I finished my work well in front of the rest of the class.

I always helped Philip, who, as I predicted the first day I met him, was to become my best friend. The fact that he was my only friend didn't matter to me. Most of the other children irritated me. I decided why should I be friendly with them when they are nasty to me. Why waste time pretending to like someone when clearly, I don't like them at all.

However, even though they annoyed me, I did like some of the girls. I can't explain why. Perhaps it is because Mother is a girl and she understands me more than anyone in the whole universe. I think girls are probably kinder than boys, there is a gentleness to them that puts me at ease.

I did eventually go to the child psychiatrist. Although, Mother said it was a total waste of time and I agree. The only advice that he gave me, was to watch myself in a mirror. When I started to pull a face or twitch my arms and legs, he advised me to concentrate hard to stop it from happening. He gave me an exam, which I finished quicker than he expected. He called it an IQ test and said that I had passed it with flying colours.

I can't understand how colours can fly. People say the strangest things to me, that don't make any sense.

Only yesterday, after P.E, the teacher said, 'Alfie, you have put your shoes on the wrong feet.'

I looked at her quizzically and said, 'But these are the only feet I have.'

She screwed her face up at me and I knew that I had said something wrong, yet again. It is as though I see the world in a different way to other people. I think I am looking through a different window. Just like on the TV programme, Playschool, that I watched when I was younger. Each day the theme was to look through a different shape window, but while everyone else is looking through the square window, I am looking through the triangle window and seeing a whole different picture.

CHAPTER FOURTEEN

Grace's Diary

14 FEBRUARY 1985

I cannot express how betrayed I felt by Paul cheating on me with that dreadful woman. I thought that Paul and I had a strong marriage. I thought Paul loved me, as I loved him. I had imagined Paul and I growing old together, enjoying our family life with Alfie and one day possibly having grandchildren. What does he see in her? When I actually laid eyes upon her that day in the playground, all kinds of thoughts went through my mind. I could not in my wildest dreams have imagined that Paul could be attracted to such a woman.

I know that I had not been myself for some time and perhaps let myself go a little in terms of my appearance, but that woman. She looked a tart. And what about her husband if she has one? What's worse, he was carrying on in front of our Alfie. Our sweet, dear boy. I hope he did not see anything that could damage his young mind.

It's Valentine's Day today, so our Pam came around and we had a girl's night in. However, instead of cheering each other up, we ended up crying. We reminisced about our lost marriages, remembering all of the good times and returning to the pain of our loss. I feel for her, her husband loved her dearly, but he tragically died. Pam's husband did not want to leave her, the choice was taken from him. He did not betray my sister. They were married according to their wedding vows. 'Till death do us part.'

Paul cheated on me, he broke our sacred wedding vows and I feel empty now. I feel lost, but I have to be strong for Alfie. I must put on a happy face and show my son that we can manage without his father. I will survive. I will become strong and independent, if only to show Paul that he has made the biggest mistake of his life.

27 MARCH 1985

The strike has ended and Paul is now living with *that woman*. Hazel came over to visit me and gently told me that she had heard that his fancy woman is pregnant. I can't believe how quickly he has moved on. However, he has been honourable and now that he is back at work he is starting to help financially. I'm worried how Alfie will feel about having a half-brother or sister.

16 APRIL 1985

When I feel angry or lonely, I always feel better if I bake. Sometimes I bake scones, butterfly cakes, or even bread. I don't have much appetite to eat it myself, but Alfie certainly does. He is growing up into a big, strong, handsome boy. I like to think that in some small way I am contributing to this, by providing Alfie with nutritious food.

My parents, when they are around and not gallivanting off to somewhere in Europe, always compliment me on my baking, which is reassuring in a small way. Pam enjoys the sweet treats too. I enjoy their visits, but they keep picking at my wounds and always talk about Paul. I wish they would just leave me alone. Each time they bring up the subject of me and Paul, it reinforces my pain.

Sometimes, after they have left me, feeling depressed, I go into the attic and get out the old photo albums. When I turn the pages and see the images of me and Paul when we were courting, I find it hard to believe that it has all gone wrong. I have deliberately avoided looking at our wedding album. I am not quite ready for that yet.

23 MAY 1985

Money is getting tight and Alfie is growing out of everything so fast. I can't keep asking Paul for money.

That dreadful woman is definitely pregnant, just as Hazel said. I am glad that she forewarned me, at least it gave me the chance to compose myself when Paul officially told me. I don't know how he expected me to behave, especially after it took me so long to get pregnant with Alfie. I hope that she is not one of those women who get pregnant every year. This will be her third pregnancy and she has loads of childbearing years in front of her. Alfie could end up with a brood of half-siblings.

I have started to slowly break the news to Alfie, however, I'm not sure if he understands. I feel for him. I want to give him the perfect life, so I spend lots of time playing with him. However, I can't bear to take him to that local playground or the swimming pool, just in case I bump into her. Maybe I will find a swimming pool in the next town to us. Otherwise, it is not fair on him to miss out on swimming because of my fear of meeting that horrible woman.

15 JUNE 1985

Now my family knows about Paul's fancy woman being pregnant. My parents seem to think that I should file for a divorce. I can't bring myself to do that yet. It is so final, so wounding.

I know that people are gossiping about Paul and he deserves it. However, he is Alfie's father and I can't help but worry in case the kids at school torment him about it. Kids can be so cruel.

2 JULY 1985

Soon it will be the school holidays. Six whole weeks to enjoy the freedom from the school run and spend quality time with Alfie. I will miss my regular visits to the Co-op, but I hope to meet up with Hazel and some of the other women after they have finished work. Next time I call in, I plan to make some definite arrangements to meet up. Perhaps we could take the children for a picnic in Sherwood Forest. It will be good for Alfie to meet other children outside of school. Perhaps, if I am close by, he might feel more confident to interact with them.

I need to find ways to keep Alfie amused without it costing me too much. I know the local library sometimes puts on events during the summer break. I will call in next week and check out the noticeboard.

22 AUGUST 1985

I can hardly believe how fast the holidays are flying by. I don't know why I was so worried; Alfie can amuse himself for ages just playing in the garden. He loves sifting through the soil, finding stones and making little piles of rubble. He spends ages washing the stones, then lining them up in colours. He made a nice little border around the edge of the lawn.

Sadly, the day out in Sherwood Forest did not go as well as I had hoped. Whilst the other children were running around pretending to be Robin Hood and Little John, Alfie sat alone and piled twigs up to make a pretend campfire. It made me feel terribly sad. Thankfully, my friends did not pass comment and neither did the children.

We've been to the library a few times and while Alfie was engrossed in art and craft sessions, I had a coffee and a chat with the other parents. I quite enjoyed our sessions at the library and have become a member. It is great. The books are free for both of us and I have read no end of books about nutrition and borrowed stacks of cookery books.

I SEPTEMBER 1985

Earlier in the month, I took Alfie out shopping for some new school clothes. He is growing so fast. Every six weeks he seems to need bigger shoes.

As a special treat, we caught the bus into Nottingham. We very rarely get the opportunity to go into the town or city centre these days. Truth be known, Alfie is not too keen on travelling by bus. He claims that they smell funny and he is probably right. I will be glad when the new railway line opens. There is talk of re-opening the old line that used to connect our village with the mainline. What a treat that would be for both of us, to catch a train direct from our old village station and into the city. Alfie has never been on a train. He has always enjoyed playing with his toy trains and watching Thomas the Tank Engine. So, it would be a real treat for him.

I felt a bit frumpy as I walked around the city centre. Most of the women my age looked so glamorous and stylish - I guess it's time I updated my wardrobe. I need to start looking for a part-time job so that I can afford a few luxuries for Alfie and myself. How wonderful that would be.

21 OCTOBER 1985

Autumn is creeping up on us and the days are getting shorter. I have been doing a lot of reading in the evenings and trying out new recipes at the weekend. It will be Halloween soon, I'm thinking of inviting Pam and my parents round to try out some of my new recipes. I have got all kinds of ideas for making scary blood looking sandwiches and spider buns. I will decorate the house with fake cobwebs and skeletons. I might even invite Hazel and her family. Alfie will be surprised. Perhaps he could invite Philip.

22 NOVEMBER 1985

Paul has a daughter - Alfie has a half-sister. My heart is aching, I feel like I can't breathe. Paul was obviously excited and wanted to introduce Alfie to his little sister Rose straight away.

Alfie asked me if Rose was more *normal* than him, for he does not want his sister to ever be as sad as he is. My heart broke into a million tiny pieces when he said this.

Paul also seemed upset and told Alfie, that in his eyes, he is just perfect the way he is. Even more so because he had been told what a little genius he had become. That was true, Alfie is incredibly clever with facts and has the ability to recall information word for word. I'm very proud of my little man.

2 DECEMBER 1985

I'm amazed at our Alfie, he is currently interested in natural history. In fact, it's an obsession. He has read every book on the subject in our local library and is now pestering me to take him to the Natural History Museum in London for Christmas. I can't bring myself to ask Paul for the extra money I need for the visit, especially now he has further financial responsibilities with his new baby. After all, Paul had been true to his word all these years supporting his son. I wonder if his fancy woman gets maintenance money for her two boys. I am well aware of how some fathers abandon their responsibilities, despite government intervention in the form of the Child Support Agency. I do hope that she gets some help from their father, otherwise, it is a massive responsibility for Paul.

25 JANUARY 1986

Alfie is more settled now. He seems to be enjoying school and providing we keep to a routine, there is no risk of a meltdown. I have decided to apply for a job vacancy that I have seen advertised at the school for a full-time cook. The hours will fit nicely around the school opening hours. During the school holidays, I will be free to spend time with Alfie. It is time I become a wage earner, I can't depend on Paul forever.

I don't know what the future for Alfie is going to be. I know that he has certain problems that will create barriers to his future, but I will never allow this to stand in his path of success. Whatever it takes, I will build up his confidence, teach him independence, and reinforce his strengths.

CHAPTER FIFTEEN

Alfie

Father has a new family and I have a sister. As soon as I looked into her eyes, I knew that she was not like me. I cannot explain how I know that, but I do. I see her clearly and I feel for her like I feel for Mother. I am going to be a good brother and when I grow up, I will look out for her and never let anyone upset her the way they try to upset me.

There are things about me that I don't like, but try as I might, these traits seem to have a life of their own. Sometimes I lie. I know I am doing it for the right reasons, but even so, it is lying and wrong. But I can't stop myself. Keeping secrets though isn't always lying. Sometimes it is the only way to protect the person you love.

The worst of it is when I lie to Mother. She so believes the best of me and refuses to believe that I could be capable of anything wicked. But I have wicked thoughts that really frighten me. They are even too bad to talk about, so I draw pictures. Dark, evil pictures and that way, the thoughts move out of my head and onto the paper. When the picture is complete, I screw it up and put it in the bin to cleanse myself of the thought.

One day, when Mother was cleaning my room, she took the screwed-up paper out of the bin and was horrified. She asked me to explain what the pictures meant and if they represent anything in particular. Mother is the only person that I feel able to talk to about anything. I know that her love for me is unconditional and that she only wants the best for me. I try and explain that the images are just that, the faces are of no one I can put a name to and the scenes are linked to some of the films I have watched on the television. I shouldn't have admitted that, as she now censors everything I watch.

Mother decided that I needed to get involved with sports instead of filling my head with too much fantasy. So, one weekend she took me to the local sports complex and enrolled me in football training. As it turned out, I was rather well placed as a goalkeeper. I am not afraid of throwing myself in any direction to save a goal. I also have the uncanny ability to work out a possible sequence of events as the strikers were heading my way.

Although I enjoy playing in the goals, I'm not a real team player, because none of the other boys liked me. They treat me with indifference, which I find very hurtful, especially as I always give my absolute best for the team in terms of saving goals. I can't say that I am upset that I'm ignored after the game, which incidentally I have helped my team to win. No, I have come to expect no less and besides, it suits me well enough to be left to my own space, with my own thoughts.

The problem is, that I can't seem to have a conversation with boys of my own age. They talk a load of rubbish compared to the older boys, who I prefer to hang around with. There are two main reasons for this. First, is that I listen and learn from them and second, their level of conversation isn't childish.

Mother seems very pleased with herself, she takes me to training twice a week and watches all of the matches. No matter what the weather is like, Mother is standing there. Sometimes in torrential rain and on freezing cold days, there she is, encouraging and supporting me with no care for herself.

Even Father comes to watch me a couple of times. He stands on the sidelines cheering me on and shouting instructions. I think me playing football has made him a little proud of me because, in all other ways, I feel that I have let him down. He hears what the other boys say about me behind my back. They really don't get me at all. I think I must be a little bit like that Marmite spread, you either love me or hate me.

Mother loves me and I think Father does. I hope one day my sister Rose will love me too. Philip is still my only friend and sometimes comes to watch me play football. He is not afraid to tell the other boys that we are friends, although he does have lots of other friends. I don't think Philip will ever forget my loyalty to him.

One particular match, I saved lots of goals and subsequently we won a great victory. Afterwards, the coach presented me with a 'man of the match trophy'. Father was there that day and was so happy with my performance, that he promised to take me to a Nott's Forest match.

It was amazing. I sat in the junior reds supporters stand and I felt part of the group. No one knew me so they didn't know that I was any different from them. I was just another supporter and provided I didn't start talking to them about things that interested me, like science and how the earth works, it was all ok.

Father had warned me not to have one-sided, intense conversations with the other supporters. He said, to just keep it simple and enjoy the day. So, that is what I did, but it was very difficult for me. I wanted to talk about the reasons why some footballs were better than others and why the ground conditions mattered. It was such a special day for my Father to take me to the match and of all the days I remember spending with him. I think I enjoyed this one the most.

I played Sunday League football for two years, winning many trophies, including man of the match and sportsman of the year. I don't understand people at times. Whilst my teammates never took to me, they were not usually unkind or cruel. However, for some reason, some of the boys began saying wicked things about me and making cruel remarks. They mimicked my facial expressions and copied the tics that I still suffered from. These strange, involuntary movements I suffered from were always worse when I felt stressed. The more they mimicked me, the more stressed I felt and the worse my tics became.

Mother said they were jealous of the awards I was winning, especially when I was offered a trial for Port Vale football club. However, I never went to the trial. Mother put a halt to the whole situation and withdrew me from the team. She told me it was for my mental health and well-being that she withdrew me.

I knew Mother had my best interests at heart and I didn't complain. She was right to withdraw me, for I was ready to punch somebody and now my body is much stronger from the sport and training, I doubt if this time it would have ended with a bloody nose.

CHAPTER SIXTEEN

Grace's Diary

16 FEBRUARY 1990

I am really enjoying my work in the school kitchens. There is no denying that it is hard work and very hot at times. I have to smile at one of the older ladies who constantly talks about her menopause problems. She is a proper character! I swear she is making up half the stories. We all share our problems, well, most of us at any rate.

My son is growing up. It is a struggle at times, although the pleasure far outweighs the pain. Paul and my family tell me that I am in denial about Alfie's behaviour and that he is not wired up like the rest of us – but I don't care what anyone thinks. My GP said that maybe Alfie has some kind of sensory processing disorder and he is being monitored. I have read some child behaviour books from the library and it appears that there is a growing number of children with behaviour like my Alfie's. I love him no matter what. He is growing into a remarkable young man, loving and kind, yet very complex on a number of levels.

14 APRIL 1990

Alfie has lots of interests, so we keep going to the library to get books on his latest obsession. Whilst he chooses his books, I pick up some books for myself too. I have started studying food science and dietetics. I hope to forge a career that will enable me to earn more money, so that I can support Alfie's future – whatever that may be. I believe in Alfie and I will guide him the best that I can, whatever path he chooses to take.

Paul tries his best to understand our son and I sometimes consider the possibility that some of the traits that Alfie has, are not dissimilar to some of Paul's behaviour patterns. However, because he is an adult, with childhood way behind him, somehow, he has managed to either overcome or disguise these traits. When I first met Paul, he stood out from the crowd. Not because of his good looks, which helped draw my attention to him that was for sure. No, it was his vulnerability, which appealed to my generous nature. He had a few close friends, but he just didn't seem to fit the group, almost like a piece of a jigsaw puzzle from the wrong box. The fact that Paul has managed to forge a good life for himself, is enough encouragement for me to hope for the same outcome for Alfie.

20 MAY 1990

Finally, I am managing to save a bit of money for the future. My wages are better than I first expected and after living quite frugally for such a long time, I seem to have got into the habit of managing my money quite well. Everyone is talking about the Costa Brava. I hear some of the women at the school gates talk about Spain and how affordable it is becoming. Even our young librarian told me that she has booked a package holiday to the Costa Brava. I am tempted to spend my savings on a holiday for me and Alfie. However, I need to be sensible. Perhaps, we can have a day trip to Skegness instead.

Alfie is not work-shy and for a while now he has kept telling me that he wants to earn some pocket money. Last week he asked me if he could try and get a paper round. I agreed on condition that it does not interfere with his schoolwork. Well, in no time at all, he secured a daily paper round with our local newsagent. It is quite close by and I know Fred the owner quite well. He is a local lad who I went to school with.

After one week, Alfie is their best young employee. Always on time and diligent with his deliveries. Everyday he slings the large bag filled with newspapers over his shoulder and rides his Raleigh Striker bike around the village. One day it rained extremely heavy, but that didn't stop our Alfie. Fred the newsagent was most impressed with his dedication.

I JULY 1990

I love the summer months, with the long days and short nights. I have been trying to get as much fresh air and sunshine as possible. I enjoy spending time in our garden after-work. The vegetables are growing nicely again this year and I have planted some outdoor tomatoes. I can't wait until they are ripe. As much as I love flowers, I can't see any point in growing them when food is more important. I planted some raspberry and gooseberry bushes last autumn. I have so much fruit, I am thinking of making some jam. I might even make some gooseberry wine.

Alfie is very careful with his paper round money, I have not seen him spend any of it yet. He says that he is saving for something special. A few days ago, he asked me if he could also take on a Sunday morning delivery too. I agreed as he seems to be really enjoying it. He is now working seven shifts in total. I think that it is good training ground for his future in terms of timekeeping and commitment. In all fairness, his time keeping is never an issue, he is most comfortable sticking to a rigid timetable. It is when things don't run to plan that Alfie gets agitated. Last week the newspapers hadn't been delivered to the shop on time and Alfie had to wait around. Fred rang me and said that he was worried about Alfie, as he became agitated and was being rude. In the end, Fred said that Alfie marched out of the shop, saying that he would be late for school. Fortunately, Fred has forgiven him. I have tried to talk to Alfie about controlling his emotions and he said that he will try a lot harder.

I saw an advert in a newspaper about the Open University and their part-time distance learning courses. I rang up and discovered that they have a food science diploma. After much deliberating, I decided that if I want to create a good future for me and Alfie, then I need to invest in myself. So, I am now a mature student. Fancy that, eh! I have read the material they have sent me and I am worried that it might be a little challenging for me, but I will persevere.

25 AUGUST 1990

Alfie really seems driven by money. Most of his friends are spending their parent's money - but Alfie wants to make money and then not spend it. He has found a new way of making money this summer holidays, he has set up a car washing business. He has been around all the local houses asking if anybody wants their car washing. I swear all the village is talking about his service. Apparently, he does a better job than the automated one at the service station.

Alfie is so obsessed with making money, that when I asked him if he wants to go on holiday to Skegness, he said no, as he did not want to let his customers down. Fancy that. A boy turning down a holiday. I am a little disappointed as I would have liked to have a holiday. Maybe next year.

I have received my first two modules and an assignment to complete before the end of October. It is so exciting, I feel like a real student.

14 NOVEMBER 1990

Alfie is at it again. Never one to miss an opportunity, he offered to clear away the leaves from people's drives and gardens, therefore earning himself extra money on top of his paper round wages. He is certainly getting plenty of fresh air and exercise. He has a huge appetite; he is a growing lad after all.

My Open University course is going well and I am enjoying learning about good nutrition and balanced diets. Every evening I set aside two hours of dedicated study time, which seems to be paying off. I got a merit for the last tutor marked assignment I sent in. I can hardly believe it myself. This is a wonderful encouragement and drives me forward to succeed with my diploma. Alfie says that he is very proud of me. I don't discuss my results with Pam, for fear that she thinks that I am bragging.

22 DECEMBER 1990

Christmas time is always awkward. Paul wants Alfie to join him on Christmas Day to open presents with Rose, but Alfie does not like that horrid woman his dad now lives with. He detests her, thank goodness. She stole my husband, stole his father. Alfie says she can't cook; her food is awful. He also complains that her Christmas decorations make his head hurt. She puts up all those neon flashing lights everywhere and ghastly tinsel. Apparently, it's chaotic there.

I'm not bitter or jealous of her anymore, I have moved on. But it's nice to know that Alfie wants to be with me at Christmas. He endures a brief trip there as he loves to spend time with his little sister. He even spent some of his money on buying her an art kit as she loves drawing.

25 DECEMBER 1990

I saved up and bought Alfie a variety of useful gifts for Christmas as he doesn't see the point of novelty items. I got him a fashionable Kappa tracksuit, a BHS jumper, gloves, and a very large accounting notebook as he loves tracking his finances.

Mum and Dad bought me some Dior Poison perfume, for when I go out on a date. I doubt that will ever happen and I am unsure if 'Poison' will attract a mate. Hazel keeps encouraging me to go out and asked if I wanted to join her and some friends on New Year's Eve. I said no, maybe when Alfie is older. I feel daft getting tarted-up. I am comfier in pyjamas and a dressing gown. I will probably celebrate New Year watching TV with a glass of Babycham.

6 JANUARY 1991

We have had lots of snow since the New Year, so Alfie has been at it again. He borrowed my snow shovel and has gone around the village making money by clearing driveways. Obviously, he recorded it all down in his book. He is a proper little accountant and a budding entrepreneur.

23 MARCH 1991

I love this time of year when new life in the earth is pushing through against all the odds. After such a terrible winter and endless snow, it is hard to believe that such delicate plants could possibly survive. It gives me hope.

My diploma studies are going fantastically well. Each time a new module arrives, I can't wait to read it. Sometimes there is an audio tape with it. I have an old Walkman cassette player that I use. I can listen for hours on end to the information about food science. I can't get enough of this fascinating subject. Each month, I send in a tutor marked assignment and a computer marked assignment, which is usually multi-choice questions. My results are always above ninety percent.

After months and months of hard work, Alfie has finally revealed to me the purpose of it all. Last week, he proudly wheeled into the kitchen a second-hand golf bag, cart and two clubs, two irons, and a pitcher. Apparently, his best friend, well, his only friend, Phillip, had asked Alfie last year to play golf with him. However, rather than ask me to buy him a golf set, he decided to do all that work to buy himself one. I am very proud of him. Every weekend Alfie and Philip go to the local golf course, Alfie looks proud as he wheels his cart down the main road. Philip is using his father's golf kit and he hopes to own his own one day.

Alfie is helping Philip to save up for his own golf kit. They have started a new business venture together. While they play golf, they keep their eyes peeled for lost golf balls, which they retrieve and clean in our back garden. Apparently, some golf balls are more valuable than others. They did some research and have made a list of the second-hand value of the different golf balls. They then sell them to the other golfers.

Paul loves sports and is apparently delighted that Alfie is interested in golf. So, Paul is going to take him out for a few rounds. I have heard that Paul likes to get out the house as much as possible these days, that fancy woman of his is apparently always nagging. Sounds familiar.

CHAPTER SEVENTEEN

Alfie

When I became a teenager, my body started to change in ways that I didn't expect. I started to grow hairs in places which had previously been smooth; the dark hair on my legs, arms, and other places seemed to grow overnight. The worst of it was on my chin and under my nose.

Father called it bum fluff, which didn't seem right to me, but I laughed with him. He said that he would buy me my first shaver for Christmas and would teach me how to shave.

Around the time I noticed the changes to my body, we started to have lessons at school about biology, which eventually helped me to understand what was happening to me. We learned about reproduction, which at first repulsed me, especially when I thought about Mother and Father copulating on a regular basis. I guess they stopped doing that after I was born, after all, the reason for doing it is to reproduce.

Thinking about it though, I guess Father must have copulated again with the woman he now lives with, because eventually they had my sister, Rose.

I never told Mother that I recognised my sister's mum, as the woman Father used to stand close to in the playground. Sometimes, I wonder if I should have told her what I had seen at the time and perhaps Father would not have left her to copulate with that other woman.

I know that Mother was very sad for a long time, but now she is like a different person. She looks pretty. Much prettier than Father's *fancy woman*, that is what my Grandmother calls her.

Sometimes I hear Mother and her father talking. He seems to think she should agree to something called a divorce so that my Father can make an honest woman of Rose's mum. It sounds like she is not to be trusted if she is not honest. Perhaps she has the same problems as me, because try as I might, sometimes I hear lies coming out of my mouth and I am unable to stop them.

Although it took me a long time and an awful lot of hard work, I saved enough money to buy my own golf bag, cart and clubs. I am proud of my kit. The bag is pale grey with a deep red and black go-faster stripe down each side. Philip helped me to choose it and the clubs and now we go together to the local golf course. It is great fun. Philip and I share the costs for a round of golf and we help to fund our next game by selling back golf balls we have found.

Some people are so stupid! Why don't they search for their own golf balls when they go missing? Perhaps they have too much money and don't care. Still, their stupidity is a good opportunity for me and Philip.

We had such a good summer together, playing golf and going on bike rides. Sometimes we went swimming or just hung around at each other's homes. Philips father was also a miner and since the problems with the strike, he had moved to a different colliery, then one day Philip told me that his father had been made redundant once again and was offered a job thirty-miles away at a colliery in Yorkshire, which meant that he and his family were moving to Yorkshire.

My one and only friend was moving away and going to a new school. I swear my heart gained weight that day it felt so heavy in my chest, almost like a cold, heavy stone.

The last day at school, I gave Philip my most treasured possession; my golf bag, cart, and clubs. I told him that now he could play with his father and remember the friendship we shared. It was one of the saddest days of my life up to that point and it took me a very long time to feel whole again.

Some days I felt very low in mood. I gave up my paper rounds and sulked around the house for days on end, listening to music and studying all kinds of scientific facts. I was interested in psychology and the way the mind works. I also liked reading about biology and was learning about how the muscles developed and became strong. Images of men who were weight training demonstrated the effects of a high protein diet on muscle mass. I became very well informed about weight training and diet, without ever stepping foot inside a gym.

Despite missing Philip, my time at the senior school, in many ways, was a good experience, I was able to mix with the older boys who I had more in common with than the boys in my school year, who I considered immature. The older lads were interested in discussing weight training and diet and asked me lots of questions, they appeared to respect my knowledge on the subject.

I know that sometimes I could also behave in an immature manner and annoy my older friends, but they laughed with me not at me, when I did something stupid. Also, for some reason, the girls liked me, perhaps it was because I treated them with respect like Mother taught me or maybe because I didn't tease and annoy them like the other boys in my form.

I definitely like girls. In fact, in many ways I enjoy being in their company more so than the boys. However, I was smart enough to know that if I spent all of my time with the girls then the name calling would start again.

There was one special girl, Janet, who I really liked. We hung around together at break-time. I think the older boys thought I was a real girl magnet, but the truth is I didn't have to try to be friends with them. It was so much easier than being friendly with the boys. I think the main reason was that there was no competition between a girl and boy, nothing to prove. Unlike the sporting competitiveness amongst the boys and the pecking order to be top dog. I didn't want to be top dog, I just wanted to be liked and accepted for who I am.

I'm not sure if the older boys that I had started to hang around with did understand me and accept me for who I was. Perhaps, I was being very naïve, for they began to encourage me to behave in ways that I knew Mother would not like.

There were lots of changes taking place in the popular culture and the music scene. Our nearest town was embracing these changes, with new nightclubs and music bars opening. My older friends had heard about one of the venues having an early session from five until nine on a Friday evening, where fourteen to eighteen-year-olds could attend. Of course, no alcohol was served, only soft drinks. However, there would be some amazing acid house music.

My older friends had already been a few times and decided it was time for me to go with them. The problem for me was how to persuade Mother to let me go. I decided this was another appropriate time to lie. Surely it would not hurt, after all, what harm could it do? How wrong was I?

Kenneth or Kenny as he preferred to be called, came to meet Mother and ask if I could go to his house for tea and to listen to some of his new music tapes after school one Friday. To be fair, Kenny put on a convincing show in front of Mother. He came smartly dressed and was most polite. Although a little wary about the situation, especially as Kenny was in the year above me at school, she agreed, providing I was home at nine o'clock. On the night in question, she trusted me with her mobile phone, a Motorola in a black leather case. I was shown how to use it to phone our landline number and advised if I got into any difficulties I was to ring home. Satisfied that all was in place for me to have a good time at my friend's house, she waved me off.

CHAPTER EIGHTEEN

Grace's Diary

17 MAY 1993

It is some time since I felt the need to write in my diary. Recent events have prompted me to once again bare my soul to pen and paper.

I should have known better, I should have gone with my instincts. Alfie's friend, Kenny, is obviously more mature than him. Although he has an easy charm about him, he is a bit too cocky and sure of himself for my liking. When I asked him for his landline number to speak with his parents, he said they were having a problem with the line and were temporarily disconnected.

However, I have since been told that Kenny has no parents. He is an orphan and lives with his older brother who is classified as his legal guardian. So, he clearly lied about the phone. It's all very tragic and almost like a TV drama, but I am angry that Alfie has been caught up in all of this. I'm just so angry. My blood is boiling. I should have known, why didn't I trust my instinct. Why?

I have just found out, that Kenny's brother is the village's biggest drug dealer and he is using his younger brother to push drugs to the local school kids. It's sick. How can this be happening in our little village? Why don't the teachers know? I am disgusted. It gets worse. I am so angry...

Last Friday, Alfie asked if he could go to Kenny's house. I was caught off guard and said yes. However, Kenny lied about his parents and they fobbed me off. I said that Alfie had to be back for nine o' clock. Well, at half-past nine, Alfie had not returned home. I began to panic and realised how stupid I was for not asking where Kenny lived.

At first, I thought that perhaps Alfie had lost track of time whilst enjoying himself. However, at ten o'clock, I rang my mobile phone. Thank goodness that I had the foresight to loan him this. I was hoping that Alfie had left it switched on. The phone certainly rang, but Alfie did not answer. I was about to contact the police when Alfie finally answered. I say answered, at first, he just sobbed and sobbed, making my heart race and my mouth go dry. Pulling myself together, I calmed him down enough to find out where he was. I guessed the phone battery was not going to last long, as I heard that dreaded beeping sound coming down the line. I desperately needed to know how to find him.

He said something about the town market. What the hell was he doing there? I told him not to move and that I was on my way. Through the sobs, I heard the word 'sorry.'

Reversing in a mad rush to turn my car around, I hit a lamp post, knocked off the number plate and scratched the bumper. I totally ignored it - I had much bigger things to worry about. Driving into town, all kinds of imaginary scenes went through my mind. Had he been in a fight and was injured? Was he drunk or drugged? Had he been robbed?

I parked as close to the market square as I could manage and ran around the disused stalls, frantically looking for Alfie. I wasn't even sure if I had heard him right. A group of drunken teenagers staggered by me with cans of cider in their hands. One of them called back to me.

'Hey, Mrs, are you looking for someone? Only, there is a lad on the floor under a stall towards the edge of the market.'

I ran like an Olympic sprinter in the direction that he was pointing. I heard Alfie before I saw him. He was curled in the foetal position under a table, sobbing and making strange, high-pitched noises. He had vomit all over his tee-shirt and his coat was nowhere to be seen. He was clutching my mobile phone underneath him, out of view of any passer-by. Where I got the strength to lift him off the ground and carry him to the car, I will never know. It was like some invisible force was giving me superpowers, parent powers, of an innate nature.

I gently laid Alfie on the back seat of the car. I checked that he was breathing ok and covered him with the blanket that I kept in the car. I was in two minds whether to take him to the emergency department at the hospital, but decided against this for fear of having to leave him there overnight without me.

I spent the whole night next to him. I turned him into the recovery position on his bed and removed his clothes. I gently washed him down and dressed him in his pyjamas. Throughout the night I constantly watched over him, turning him from side to side every two hours and wetting his lips. He vomited twice and each time I saved him from choking. He wet the bed without even realising, while his young body trembled and shook as though he was having an epileptic fit.

In the morning Alfie's eyes were bloodshot and swollen, his lips were cracked and dry and his tongue sore and furred. I helped him up the bed and supported him with pillows, passed him a drink and advised him to sip it slowly. It wasn't the right time for interrogation, that could wait, no matter how impatient I was to know the truth. Luckily it was Saturday, so I had the whole weekend to take care of Alfie. I wondered if I should have told Paul about what happened, but foolishly thought that I could manage this alone.

Alfie was very hungry for sweet and sugary foods, managing to eat a large amount of carbohydrate foods throughout the day. Around six o'clock I was exhausted and unable to keep my eyes open. By this time Alfie was looking much better, although a little twitchy and his tics were worse than usual. After a long soak in the bath, I made us both some warm milk, then sat beside him on the sofa.

He watched a repeat episode of Top of the Pops. The stage was full of young people dressed in the strangest of coloured clothes, moving their limbs about erratically to what Alfie described as acid house music.

I told him that it was time to talk and promised him that I was willing to hear what he had to say, providing that he gave me honest answers.

He told me that he had never planned to go to Kenny's house, that it was just an excuse to be allowed out in the evening so that he could go to the teenage nightclub in town that everyone his age was going to. All of the time Alfie spoke to me, he held his head down. I interpreted this as shame. In reality, it was because he was lying.

He said that his older friends had encouraged him to drink some of the coke they had managed to hide down their big, baggy trousers. It had been very hot and noisy so he was glad of the drink and very quickly finished the whole can. Shortly afterwards, he said that he felt unwell and needed to sit down. It appeared he remembered nothing from then until he woke up in his own bed.

The story that Alfie spun me was designed to distract me from the truth. He was willing to make up lies about inadvertently drinking huge amounts of alcohol, but was too ashamed of the real reason that he put himself at so much risk that night. I have now found out that he took drugs.

My son took drugs. I thought he was different to that. I thought that he was immune to such behaviour. He likes to make money, not spend it on disgusting things. Drugs!

I am so angry and ashamed. How could he do this to me? How could he do it to himself?

I have such a lot going on in my life at present, what with my studies and a full-time job. Thank goodness for this diary, which is turning more into a journal than anything. It is helpful for me to write down all of my worries, this way I don't burden anyone else. Besides, my parents would not understand and I don't wish to worry them.

CHAPTER NINETEEN

Alfie

Hanging around with Kenny and the rest of his mates is cool. They treat me as one of the lads. They don't seem to notice that I'm not quite like the other boys. This makes me feel almost normal and accepted for who I am, without any pressure or prejudice.

Kenny has an older brother who often meets him outside of the school gates and regularly passes him a small parcel. Kenny calls it a wrap. After a few weeks of noticing this I asked Kenny what was in them, he told me that he sells sweets to the older guys at school as a way of making money so that they could pay their bills. Sometimes Kenny hung around for a long time after school. Far too long for me to keep him company, but he never objects when I need to go home.

He just says, 'Cool Alf. Off you go, you lucky bugger. I expect your mam has a nice hot meal ready for you.'

He never really spoke about his parents or how they died. I guess it was too painful for him. Although I very rarely see my Father these days, at least I know he is around. I feel certain that if things got really bad for whatever reason, Father would help. I know he would.

Kenny and his brother have only each other. That must be so difficult for them both and yet, most of the time, they appear quite happy, even to the point of being silly at times.

Kenny and his friends had started to go to an acid house club in town that opened early for us teeny boppers as his older brother called us. After a Friday session at the club, I never saw Kenny until Monday morning at school, when he enjoyed nothing better than describing the whole music scene and trying to encourage me to go with them one Friday.

I told him that Mother would never let me go, not knowingly anyway. My lies were by now becoming second nature. So, we had no trouble in fabricating a story to convince her that I was having a meal at Kenny's and just hanging around listening to music.

Word must have got around about the venue in town having an early session for us teeny boppers. The queue outside of the club was the longest I have ever seen. Full of lads all dressed in their baggy trousers and Joe Bloggs tops.

The girls had very little on at all and were dressed up like mini models. Covered in make-up, with hair so big and earrings so long that it is any wonder, they could hold up their tiny heads. The atmosphere was electric. When the double doors opened to the sound of synthesised music blasting through the street, the sway of the crowd pushed us into a huge, dark room full of flashing lights and strange neon beams. Fibre optic lamps were set on tables in the corners of the room. Except for a few high stools, there was no seating. Everyone was standing, bouncing up and down to the music, waving their hands and screaming. Some of the kids had whistles around their neck, every so often they would blow them loudly. Scattered around the room, I saw raised arms waving glow sticks, neon coloured lights bobbing around to the beat, like a brightly lit fairground. It was deafening and yet exhilarating at the same time.

I saw Kenny work his way around the kids, giving them sweets. I think they paid him for the sweets, but it was all done very discreetly. The bottle of water that he'd told me to bring didn't last long. It was really thirsty work, jumping up and down to the music and waving my arms in the air to the backbeat. Everyone seemed to be full of life and energy, but within an hour I was flagging and very thirsty. Above the noise, I shouted to Kenny to get me a drink. What he gave me tasted funny but I was so thirsty I gulped it down within seconds. Kenny looked worried and told me to sit down.

That was not easy, there was very little room and I was so hot. I tugged off my jacket and threw it on a pile of coats that was on the floor close to the door. My head began to feel strange, kind of numb and I felt as though I wanted to sleep, but that meant that I would miss out on all the fun. Everyone else was still full of energy. I tugged at Kenny's trousers and told him that I was disappointed that I wasn't joining in the fun. So, he gave me one of his sweets, which seemed to do the trick.

My body was electric like I was supercharged. Not sure when or how I left the venue. I vaguely remember needing some fresh air, then looking for somewhere to lay down. Seems like I found a nice market stall to lie under, then as if like magic I somehow woke up in my own bed. How weird was that?

It took me the entire weekend to feel anything remotely like normal. Mother never left me alone for the whole two days and on Monday morning I was half expecting her to walk me to school. How embarrassing that would have been? The thing is, she now knows of the lies that I am capable of telling her, so somehow, I need to find a way of regaining her trust. It is not going to be easy. However, I have made a start my accepting that I am now grounded for a whole month, which means no hanging around after school and no time with the lads at the weekend down at the local park. Mother seems to think, that I had been drinking alcohol, but now I have begun to realise what the sweet was that Kenny gave me. I heard some of his friends talking about me while they were stood behind me in the assembly a few days later. I don't know if it was on purpose or not, but I sure am grateful for finding out.

Kenny had given me an 'E' tablet and it sure did work. However, the water infused with alcohol apparently reacted with the tablet, which is why I was so unwell and out of it. I am grounded now. It will be some time before I get the opportunity to go clubbing again. However, when I do go, I am going to ask Kenny for an E at the beginning of the night. Only this time I will know what to expect.

Talk got around the school, as it does, that I had been found by my Mother following an overdose of drugs after a wild time at a nightclub. At first, I was most annoyed by the exaggerated story, however, it had a flip side. All of a sudden, I became a minor celebrity amongst my own year group. Everyone wanted to be my friend, they wanted to know what the club was like and what kind of music was played. But most of all they wanted to know about the alcohol and drugs. Even though I wasn't allowed to hang with Kenny after school, there was no way to stop me joining up with him at break times, which is exactly what I started to do.

On the first day back at school, Kenny caught up with me at lunch break. He winked at me and asked how it felt to be one of the bad guys. I hadn't thought of myself as a bad guy. For me the fact that I was different from most kids of my age group was tough enough. I started joining Kenny and his mates behind the science block, which was pretty remote. There never seemed to be much activity in the science department. We sat around and smoked. Sometimes Kenny brought us some 'skunk' weed to add to the tobacco. He said his brother gave it to him for services rendered.

Whatever that meant. By the time my period of grounding was up, we had reached the six-week summer holidays. Normally I would look forward to this, but this time was an exception. Mother had the whole six weeks planned out for me and there was never an opportunity to catch up with Kenny.

When I returned to school, Kenny did not return. I later learned that he had died of a heroin overdose and his brother was arrested and put in prison for dealing drugs. This really shook me up, spiralling me into depression. My tics became uncontrollable and I was having paranoid thoughts.

Mother took me to see the doctor, who wasn't very helpful at all. He talked about me as though I wasn't in the room. Mother was pressing the doctor for a diagnosis. I could have told them both what my problem was, but I left them guessing. Truth was, my paranoia was directly linked to the skunk I had been smoking with Kenny. I wasn't able to relax, my body was constantly in fight or flight mode and I needed to learn how to cope, so I threw myself into my studies.

Mother was most impressed when I started watching the classics on film, for my English literature studies. To be honest, I grasp the plot better when I watch the film production as opposed to reading the book. I can become totally absorbed by a film. I think my brain responds better to visual learning than listening to endless lectures from teachers.

I didn't take the first year of my GCSE's seriously. To be honest, I wasn't very interested in any of the subjects, even though I had chosen the best of a bad bunch. We had to study English language and literature, mathematics, and combined science. In addition, we were encouraged to choose one of the humanities. Difficult decision. The thing about GCSE's is that so much emphasis was placed on the coursework, which meant that even after school, I was expected to continue with my studies. I suppose that

I was lucky in some respects, as Mother took a real interest in the work I was doing and helped as much as possible.

A video rental shop opened in our village and was rapidly becoming popular with the local families. All kinds of popular films were available to borrow and the shelves were full of mainstream films. I was desperate for Mother to buy a video recorder so that I could watch some of the latest films and chat with the lads at school about the heroes and villains. To my surprise, one Saturday afternoon, my dream came true. Although it was second-hand, my grandparents had managed to purchase a half decent recorder from one of the guys at the Welfare Club who was apparently having a few money problems. Poor bloke, I think Grandfather drove a hard bargain. Now we had a video recorder, Mother was able to rent some videotapes to help with my English literature. She loaned some educational videos from the local library, they had quite a collection of the classics. We sat and watched a production of Hamlet over and over again and when there was a production on at the Theatre Royal in Nottingham she took me there. It was brilliant.

The poetry was a bit tricky to study. It was a collection by William Blake so Mother encouraged me to make a tune to go along with the verse. I imagined a beat to the words, which really helped. By the second year of my GCSE's I decided to pay proper attention to the subjects, learning most things word for word. I could remember whole chunks of information and didn't really make notes in class. While most of the students in the class could be seen frantically scribbling notes, I read and memorised whole chunks of information. Very often, I was reprimanded during class for not taking notes. However, when the teacher asked questions at the end of class, fully expecting me to not have a clue, I always enjoyed seeing the disappointed look on their face when I was able to answer the question. It was the same in science, especially chemistry.

The teachers tried to catch me out, because I had not written the formula in my notebook, on many occasions I was passed a piece of chalk and asked to write a given formula on the blackboard. This was not an issue as I could remember complex sequences and patterns.

I must admit though; my writing style is shameful. I never seem to be able to write in a straight line and there is no uniformity in the size of my letters. Most of the time I write large letters, but some ridiculously so. When I look at the words that I have written from a distance, even I recognise that a five-year-old could probably have done a better job. I guess that my brain is firing off quicker than my hands can write, so I compensate by writing in a style that is eligible but only just.

My overactive and complicated mind is occasionally advantageous, but most of the time it just makes me different from the others. Not that it is obvious to people who have just met me, but very soon after, they begin to realise that I am not wired up the right way. Sometimes, I feel that half of me is normal, but the other half is not. It is very confusing. I can only describe myself as having two personalities. I'm not saying that I am psycho, a schizoid, or even that I have a split personality. No, it is as though I have two sides to me that don't appear to fit together, although I am one person.

Maths was a totally different entity. I wasn't able to memorise maths, only the formula. This needed lots of practice. Father came in very useful with maths, apparently, he was better with numbers than words. So, once a week I went to his home and we sat comfortably together practising for my exams. I say comfortable in a loose kind of way. His new wife appeared to possess no house-keeping skills whatsoever. The house was always a total mess, cluttered and untidy. In all of the times I have visited I have never seen the kitchen sink minus a pile of greasy pots. Father always needs to make a space on the kitchen table so that we can work together. We sit at the table surrounded by piles of washing, some clean and some disgustingly filthy. I don't know how Father puts up with such slovenly conditions. To say that it is not very clean is an understatement. I try and avoid using the bathroom at all costs.

My sister, Rose, is growing into a very lovely little girl. She is always fussing around me when I visit, showing me her own school work and the pictures she has drawn. Rose loves animals and draws lots of pictures of horses, dogs, and cats. Actually, her drawing skills are quite astounding for her age. She told me that she goes horse riding and one day wants to work on a farm. I don't know what work I want to do and I am much older than Rose.

I think, if I pass my GCSE exams, I might stay at school for two more years and study A-levels. Perhaps by then, I will know what kind of work I am qualified to do, or more to the point, suitable to accomplish. The closer my exams, the more stressed and anxious I became and the more my tics became noticeable. Mother had recently relaxed about me going out and had allowed me to go to the local youth club with a group of boys from my class. She knew some of their parents and had approved the boys. But us boys can be very deceptive. The truth was, that we all had baggy trousers with deep pockets and it was easy to persuade one of the older boys to get us some cans of White Lightning cider from the supermarket.

I wouldn't say that they were my friends. We just hung out together, listened to the same music and tried to chat the girls up. I never had any problem in that department. Apparently, I am a good dancer and the weird thing is, my tics disappear when I dance. The White Lightning cider helps me to relax and chase away the many ideas and thoughts that swim around inside my overactive mind. Some of my thoughts are totally crazy. For example, I think about the manner in which this youth club is managed. There are so many possibilities for improving it. The club must be losing so much money and can't possibly be sustained in its current state. Father told me that the NCB, that is the money from the mines, sponsor the local youth activities. Well, I don't think the money is being used sensibly.

Whenever I go to the youth club, chances are I will be walking home with a girl attached to my arm. Some weeks there is live music on at the senior youth club and the bands are quite good. I wouldn't mind learning to play the guitar, maybe the base. I can visualise myself sat cross-legged on the floor, broodily strumming a tune, looking cool and moody. Perhaps when my GCSE's are over I might have a few lessons. It was certainly something to look forward to, although Mother expects me to get a job the moment my exams are completed. She is right, of course, if I am going to university I will need lots of books and other essentials to help me get by. Maybe I can get a second-hand guitar from one of the many car boot sales that seem to be popping up everywhere.

CHAPTER TWENTY

Grace's Diary

25 FEBRUARY 1994

I have not written since that dreadful incident. I am still shocked and scared that I could have lost my boy that night. My sweet boy, who is growing up so fast. I think the incident scared him and he has changed. Alfie appears to be settling down to some serious study. I am very proud of the way he manages to overcome some of the difficulties he endures, related to his psychological issues. In general, I can see when he is beginning to feel stressed, his tics become much more noticeable and his eyes have a distant look about them. Although he is growing tall, he does not seem to be developing the muscle mass of his peer group. I have also noticed that his gait is a little unusual.

I have not yet discussed this with him, for I fear he has enough to contend with. I have decided that when he has completed his exams next year, perhaps I can get some extra work on the weekend in order to afford a membership to the local sports centre. Perhaps if he has a personal trainer and does some weight training then just maybe he will develop stronger muscles.

Although I am working long hours to support us, I have discouraged Alfie from taking on a part-time job. I know that he is more than willing to earn his own pocket money, but so much relies on him getting good exam results. His future and to some extent my own depends on him getting a well-paid job. One thing is for certain, my son is not going down the mine like Paul.

CHAPTER TWENTY-ONE

Alfie

What a relief, the exams are over. I tried my best and now, along with all of my peer group, we have to wait and agonise over the results. Some of the lads have invited me down to the local sports complex, for a game of football and a few drinks after to celebrate. Apparently, it is a long-held tradition to get drunk after the exams. Well, I am up for that. Of course, it won't be easy, sneaking in by Mother so I will have to play my cards right.

Luck was with me. On the evening in question, Mother was to attend an evening work meeting. She had made arrangements for me to go to my grandparents for tea after school. She told them that I had permission to go out with the lads for a game of football, after which I was to go home and shower. My grandparents had arranged to call around at nine-thirty to check on me. I couldn't have planned it better myself.

I had a great time playing in the goals, showing my skills. Truthfully, sometimes I think that is the basis for being invited out as part of the group. As well as the fact the lads think that I am a girl magnet, something they take advantage of. I'm not sure what their problem is. I never have any issues talking to the girls and sometimes I think that I am more on their wavelength than I am the boys. Whatever the reason, it appears that I have some kind of charisma. Lucky me!

After the game, some of the older lads joined us around the changing rooms. They had a huge supply of alcohol, including White Lightning Cider and Mad Dog 20/20. One of the lads had a Coca-Cola bottle, which he claimed was mostly vodka with a bit of cola. He offered to sell it to us for a tenner. Four of us clubbed together and took it off his hands. We sat and fooled around for a couple of hours. The alcohol appeared to have a profound effect on some of the lightweights, who left early, the worse for wear. There was only three of us left, to finish the vodka, which was really helping me to relax.

I could feel a calmness, such as I have never experienced before. The worries I had about not being wired up right seemed to be a distant memory. As I chilled with the lads, I felt like one of them and not a psycho, as I have been so often called.

Not sure what the time was. I vaguely remember being joined by the same lads who had sold us the alcohol earlier in the evening. By this time, our bottle was nearly empty. I was feeling so good, relaxed, and chilled, so I accepted a bottle of White Lightning for a small cost. I rested my head against the wooden veranda of the changing hut and drank the whole bottle. At some point, I heard a commotion and noticed the other lads running off, but I was not able to move. My body felt as though it would float away into the distance, taking my unusually calm mind with it. I felt myself being lifted from the floor and carried somewhere. I think it was a van. In between sharp slaps on my face, I must have given them my name and address. After that, everything went blank.

CHAPTER TWENTY-TWO

Grace's Diary

1 JULY 1994

Being a parent is bloody hard work. I feel like an emotional wreck most of the time. How can they put us through this trauma? Sometimes I feel so alone and I can't breathe. Don't get wrong, being a mother is wonderful but also scary. It's like an emotional roller coaster. Thank goodness, I get to write my feelings in this diary. I don't know what else I would do; perhaps go crazy?

So, what has Alfie done this time? Well, I was still in a meeting when I felt my mobile phone vibrate in my pocket. I told Alfie to only call me in an emergency, so I was on full alert, made my excuses and left the room.

My Father spoke to me in an agitated voice, briefly informing me that we had a situation and I needed to get back to their flat as soon as possible. I was forty minutes' drive away from my parents, but managed it in thirty minutes. God knows how many red lights I jumped or how many other risks I took but I was on a mission. My son needed me.

I found Alfie, flat on his back, only partially conscious on my parent's bed. Sick dribbled from his mouth. I couldn't believe how stupid my parents were. I was horrified at their ignorance and immediately asked Dad to help me get Alfie onto his side. Mum helped me wash him down and remove his clothes, replacing them with my father's old, checked dressing gown.

I sat beside my beloved son and held his hand, telling him not to be afraid as I would take care of him, no matter what.

Dad reluctantly told me that the police had found Alfie at the sports complex. His so-called mates had run off, leaving him to take the blame. They were going to take him to the hospital until he gave them our address. Unfortunately, it was our home address and when the police went to the door and no one answered. They went to the adjoining house, where my very good neighbour, Sheila, gave them my parents' address. Apparently, she told them that I was a good mother and likely he was under my parents' supervision. Thank goodness for Sheila.

My parents said they were shocked when they answered the door to the police. Their immediate thought was that I had been involved in an accident. Their shock, however, turned to anger, when they were informed of the real reason. I truly believe that they were more worried about what their neighbours think than how ill Alfie was. Mum said that the neighbour's curtains were twitching and she had never felt more embarrassed.

Embarrassed indeed! This was their grandson and he needed help, and I need emotional support. What is wrong with them? Isn't it enough that they selfishly spent all their savings travelling the world without a care for their old age.

I rang Paul in the end, as my parents were being useless and judgemental. I can't remember the last time that I asked him to help me and was thankful that he did not let me down. He came thirty minutes later and carried Alfie in his arms, gently laying him on the back seat of his car. I followed Paul back to my house. I am very grateful to Paul.

Sometimes I wonder, should I have forgiven him for his affair with that woman? Should I have tried harder to make our marriage work? It is so hard and exhausting being a single parent. It's like an emotional roller coaster, nothing prepares you for the highs and lows of parenting. Cleaning sick from your drunk teenager son is definitely a parenting low.

I wanted Paul to divorce me and he finally did. However, I feel so lonely at times. Could I have made it work with Paul? Should I have fought harder? So many thoughts whirling around inside my head.

Oh, Alfie. Why did you do this to me again?

I nursed him through the night. I think he may have had alcohol poisoning. I hope that he hasn't damaged his young liver. What if he suffers long-term consequences?

When Alfie felt better, he became extremely remorseful. I spent ages talking to him about the dangers of excessive alcohol consumption. Alfie is very literal and matter of fact, so we went to the library and we picked up lots of biology books. I am going to sit down with him and together we can research the effects of alcohol on the body.

AUGUST 1994

Alfie received his GCSE exam results and we are absolutely delighted that he passed every subject as predicted. He even got A-stars in science, English, and history. Even so, I grounded him for the first week of the summer holidays and we spent it studying biology and the effects of alcohol on the body. He seems very interested in how the human body works. I have used the skills that I have obtained from my Open University diploma and together we are studying the anatomy and physiology of the liver and the hepatic portal system. We also studied the kidneys and the process of excretion.

Alfie is like a sponge, he just soaks up all the information in an incredible way. I believe this has helped him decide the route he wants to pursue for his future. He is going to do his A-levels at sixth form school and has chosen biology as one of his subjects. He even surprised me and said his long-term goal is to attend university and study something in medicine, depending on his A-level grades. Two more years of study. I am already fifty-one years of age and feeling more tired with every passing day.

Alfie is aware of the financial implications and so he said that he will get a weekend job during term time and a full-time position during the holidays. How could I argue with him, there would be no other way? Also, it will keep him out of mischief.

We celebrated his GCSE results at Antico Italian restaurant. Whilst there, Alfie confidently approached the manager, Mr Rossi and inquired about employment. I was pleasantly surprised when Mr Rossi said yes straight away and informed him he could start the next day as someone had just quit.

Whilst I was sipping my coffee and eating dessert in the restaurant, I caught sight of a pale looking girl with jet black hair walk past me. She looked very serious, and different to the other heavily made-up jovial waitresses. I wonder how Alfie will fit in working in Antico's. It's very different from his paper round and selling golf balls. Still, it's a good starting point and he has proved that he has a good head for business. I think he made a fair bit of money from his car washing enterprise.

CHAPTER TWENTY-THREE

Alfie

The school holidays are too long. The whole concept of having six weeks break from study is counterproductive in my opinion. I get it that the teachers need a break. After all it must be a nightmare controlling a bunch of kids all day, especially the ones who don't want to learn. Most of the time I am okay with school. I quite enjoy the set routine, the timetable, and the rules. However, occasionally I see the absurdity of trying to teach students who have no intention of learning.

Here is the thing; I have every intention of becoming successful. I don't mean working forty hours a week to make someone else rich, all that bourgeoisie and proletariat nonsense. No, I will find a way to make big money. Not just enough to pay the mortgage and have an annual holiday. I aim for much more. Watch this space.

My current wages are a joke. In fact, along with the other young waiters, I think I am being exploited. However, I am learning social skills and observing the behaviour of the workforce, something that can't be read about in a book.

One of the waitresses is amazing. She stands out from the rest, not because she is exceptionally pretty or has the biggest breasts or even the longest legs. Magenta is outstanding because she is not afraid to be different. I admire her for being true to herself and not conforming to society's expectations.

Magenta has amazing shiny black hair, cut just like Queen Cleopatra in the history books. Instead of the repulsive orange make-up that most of the girls wear, she has the palest of skin. It's almost ivory, and she wears a lipstick shade which is so dark it is almost black. She is fascinating.

Her eyes are green with flecks of hazel swirling around and her lashes are incredibly long. Most of the girls wear short, skimpy skirts, covered with a white frilly apron. Not her. Oh no. Magenta wears a black, clingy, maxi skirt which shows off her amazing figure. Instead of a white frilly apron, she wears a long black apron tied off at the front. To be honest, when we work the same shift I find her quite distracting.

One evening, the boss suggested that we finish early as it was not at all busy. I guess he didn't want to pay us for hanging around, which was fair enough but not good for my pocket. Some of the staff were talking about going into town and trying to get into one of the pubs that was known to be a bit loose on the rules. I was all set to take a pass on the idea when Magenta grabbed my hand and declared that we were both up for it. What could I say, this goddess had spoken and no way was I going to argue.

I had the most enlightening evening of my life to date. The conversation was unlike any conversation that I had so far encountered with any group of young people. We actually had an intelligent conversation about social injustice, religion and politics. Makes a change from the usual banal topics of football, fashion, and who was shagging who.

Although we were only together for part of the evening I began to feel a connection with Magenta and it turns out she felt the same way. Magenta and I have spent most of the school holidays hanging out. She is a huge believer in Paganism and alternative medicine. Everything about her feels magical and surreal. I have been so influenced under her spell that I have completely surrendered myself to the gothic movement that Magenta embraces. It is quite liberating wearing the goth clothes and hanging out with the crowd. For the first time ever, I feel that I belong to a group. I am not on the outside looking in. I have been accepted for who I am.

The first time Magenta visited my home, with Mother's super tidy ways and almost military-style tactics, it occurred to me what contrasting lives we lead. Yet these superficial differences have no bearing on who we really are. For me, the most important aspects of a good relationship, are mutual love and respect. We should respect one another's differences, this is something that my Mother always taught me. I knew she would be surprised at the way Magenta dressed, however, I know that my Mother will see beyond the clothes.

Thankfully, Mother did not let me down in any way at all. She welcomed Magenta into our home, making no fuss and putting her immediately at ease. However, there was one slight problem. I forgot to mention that Magenta is a vegan and Mother prepared a magnificent spread of food, the majority of which was not suitable for her. Poor Mother was horrified, but being an experienced, innovative cook, she quickly remedied the problem, which greatly impressed Magenta.

CHAPTER TWENTY-FOUR

Grace's Diary

SEPTEMBER 1994

Life is good. I feel that we are finally moving forward and there is no drama. The summer holidays went well and Alfie was on his best behaviour. He is working hard at Antico's and is saving up his money for when he goes to university.

When he does the evening shift, I meet up with Hazel or my sister and I have a girls' night out. However, I can't drink, as I have to drive and pick Alfie up from work. Still, it is good to socialise even if it is only at the local pub.

On a nice evening, I really enjoy sitting outside in the garden chatting with Hazel. It's so good to have a friend to chat and laugh with. She is a bit of a gossip at times though and is always telling me some of the secrets going on in the village. She told me that Kenny's older brother has been locked up again for drug dealing. I will never forgive him for how many lives' he messed up. A very tragic family. Thank goodness, I removed Alfie from his company before any further harm was done.

Pam keeps asking me if I want to go downtown with her to meet some *eligible gentleman friends*, as she calls them. I don't like the idea of getting tarted-up and going to a busy bar where I get looked at like I am a piece of meat. Paul broke my heart and I want to focus on my studies now and a future career. I don't want to go bringing any men into my life and complicating it further. Alfie and I are getting along so well. However, I am starting to wonder about his love life.

He has started to share interesting snippets of conversations with me about the customers, especially the rude and complaining ones. He has even started talking about one of the waitresses. This is the first time ever that he has talked to me about girls. Her name is Magenta. I have no idea what her parents were thinking of calling her that. It's a bit fancy for our village. Whenever he discusses Magenta, I get the impression that just maybe, the feeling is mutual. With this in mind, I have encouraged him to invite her for a meal one evening so that I can meet her. You never know, maybe she will become my daughter-in-law one day.

OCTOBER 1994

I have finally met Magenta. Last Sunday, after he finished his lunchtime shift, Alife came bounding into the kitchen holding hands with an outstandingly pretty girl. Alfie didn't introduce her, but I knew it was Magenta. She has ebony black hair cut into a severe bob and the palest face that I have ever laid eyes upon in the living world. She was dressed from head to toe in black. However, what caught my attention the most, is the metal ring through her lip and her thick, black eyebrows.

At first, I was shocked and then realised that I had seen her before. She was in the restaurant the night we celebrated Alfie's exam results. I wonder if Alfie had noticed her that night and that was why he applied for a job there? Hmm. Very interesting.

I was pleasantly surprised that Magenta shook my hand, gazed into my eyes and greeted me with the most amazing smile. I was quite taken back.

Magenta definitely has breeding; her accent and the delivery of her words speak volumes. I actually felt self-conscious about my own accent and use of vocabulary. Alfie, bless him, apologised for not giving me notice and asked if it was ok for Magenta to stay for tea. Of course, I said yes.

They spent the entire afternoon and most of the evening in Alfie's room, only surfacing for food and drinks, which they promptly took upstairs with them. I suppose I should be worried about leaving two hormonal teenagers alone in the privacy of a bedroom. Yet for some reason, I get the impression that Magenta is a sensible girl, despite her unique dress sense and piercings.

I did quietly sneak upstairs and listen at the door. They appeared to be talking about philosophy, something Alfie has never shown any interest in before. I guess us women have a way of engaging the male mind away from thoughts other than sex, a subject that so far, I have not had the desire to discuss with my son. I guess it is time that I had a talk about the birds and the bees.

MARCH 1995

I have been extremely busy over the last six months because I signed up for an international cookery course at the local college. I feel like Delia Smith. I really enjoyed the Indian food lesson and started chatting with the teacher, Sunita, who I am going to meet for a coffee.

I have been cooking some vegan Indian food for Alfie and Magenta, they seem to really enjoy it. They spend lots of time together talking about philosophy. I was quite intrigued, so I have borrowed *The Age of Reason* by John-Paul Satre from the library to try and understand what they are talking about.

One day, Hazel came over for a coffee and laughed when she saw I was reading Satre. She said her colleagues at the Co-op are fans of Mills & Boon. She didn't know anyone who reads anything so heavy.

Sometimes, I feel that my son is expanding my horizons and through him, I am actually seeing into different worlds. He is becoming extremely intelligent and cultured. Most of the lads round here have never understood him and now there is even less chance, such is his level of knowledge compared to most of the local lads. The majority of the young men in our village, follow their father down the mines. Some get an apprenticeship and in doing so, get the opportunity to go to the local technical college. I often think about Philip and his family. I do hope that Philip settled in his new home. Maybe one day Alfie will make contact with him again. I do hope so.

CHAPTER TWENTY-FIVE

Alfie

Magenta really gets me. She understands and accepts me for who I am. My imperfections she describes as quirky behaviour, not unlike her own. Most people find my conversation too intense and heavy. The truth is, they clearly don't understand a word I am saying. Yet Magenta appears to understand me and speak my kind of language.

Sometimes I feel that I am speaking a foreign language to other people and until I met her. I was beginning to think that nobody would ever understand me. Other people view Magenta as weird, this is so untrue. She is being true to herself, expressing herself through her art and literature. Mags as I call her is very knowledgeable about philosophy. We have in-depth discussions about Nietzsche and Jean-Paul Satre, as well as the ancient Greek philosophers.

We try and spend as much time as possible together, mostly at my house. Mags never talks about her family. The first time that I enquired about them, I noticed a pained expression on her face. So, I never brought up the subject again. For the same reason, I never asked about going to her place at the weekends.

Mother seems very happy for us to spend our free time at my house. She is very accommodating and does not ask too many questions. Although I guess she is also wondering about Mag's family. I know that she has two younger sisters who she sometimes mentions, I think she worries about them for some reason.

Although Mags and I go to different schools on the opposite side of town, we always manage to meet up on the weekends. Mags goes to a Catholic school. Turns out her family are very religious, something she constantly battles against. I guess she probably has to dress down her goth image at home, it must cause a lot of trouble for her.

She once allowed me to see her without her white face make-up and black lips. I watched with interest as she used a baby wipe to remove her make-up, followed by the removal of her earrings and piercings. Actually, Mags looked so fresh and lovely. However, there was a sadness on her face that day. Her eyes looked so sad and haunted. She almost appeared afraid.

Turns out, she always removes her gothic image before going home. What I never understood was how she managed to leave the house as a goth and return as a pseudo-Catholic girl?

Both of us secured a permanent Saturday evening job at Antico Restaurant, enabling us to enjoy the whole day and evening together. Mother insists I spend my Sundays at home, to catch up on my A-level coursework, which is going extremely well. Currently, I am studying maths, physics, chemistry and biology with a view to going to university to study pharmacology. Mags is studying the humanities, including law. She appears to have a passion for helping less fortunate people, the vulnerable who are desperate for a voice. I worry about her at times. She can be more intense than me, which takes some beating. She once told me that sometimes, the loneliest place in the world is slap bang in the middle of a crowd and that is how she felt at home.

We were halfway through the first year of A-level studies when I first noticed the bruises on her wrists. As usual, Mags dismissed them as being of no consequence and not wishing to pursue the subject any further, I let the subject drop. However, I did keep a watchful eye on my precious Mags.

Some Sundays, Mother invited Mags to join us for dinner. Always she prepared a variety of vegan food, knowing Mags' preferred tastes. Over time, both Mother and I had noticed that Mags was not looking well. She appeared to be losing weight and her hair was dull, not the shiny ebony of six months previous.

One such Sunday, Mother gently enquired if things were alright at home. At first, she did not answer. Mags held her head down and without a spoken word, she began to cry. Within seconds I was by her side, drawing her head towards my chest and gently cradling her in my arms.

Mags sobbed and sobbed. In between the sobs she tried to speak. The only words she kept repeating was, 'I could not stop him, I could not save her.'

Mother encouraged me to take Mags upstairs to my room for a rest. To be truthful, I felt out of my depth with the situation, so I did as I was told.

It took Mags a long time to gain control of her emotions, by which time, her lovely face was streaked with black mascara running down her puffy face. I called to Mother for some wet wipes. With trembling hands, Mags cleaned her face of make-up. Sadly, she could not wipe away the stress in her young face. Mother was only too pleased to be of help and insisted that Mags had a nice, long, relaxing soak in the bath. She even lit an aromatherapy candle, provided Mags with her very best toiletries. Afterwards, she insisted on driving her home. At first, she resisted, but I guess she didn't have the strength to argue as she gently nodded her head.

I had never been to her home and had no idea that she lived in the better part of the town. As we approached a very impressive detached property, I observed Mags' whole body tense. I held her shaking hand, it felt cold and clammy. My Mags was very afraid of something and I guessed it had some connection with her family.

As Mother pulled onto the long, winding drive leading to the house, Mags turned towards me and stroked my cheek.

'Always remember me, Alfie, for I will never forget you.'

She took me by surprise, I was not expecting that. Her words were so final, so wounding that no way was I going to let her go alone to the house. I could not figure it out. When Mags opened the door of the car, I was right behind her.

She shot me a warning look, then with a pleading voice told me to go back to the car, but it was too late. The impressive front door was abruptly opened and there stood her father and what a brute he looked. He stood at least six feet five inches tall. He reminded me of a pugilist with his squashed battered face and bull-like neck. Christ, was he vocal. With alarming speed, he grabbed Mags forcefully dragging her towards the open door. He slapped her hard across the face, forcing her to lose her footing. Then he grabbed her by the collar of her coat, lifting her off the ground.

Although I couldn't match him in size, youth was on my side. I made my way to the open door ahead of him, blocking the entrance with my own body. I pressed the whole weight of my body against the door and kept it ajar by sprigging my foot against the bottom rim.

'What the hell do you think you can achieve, you, young whippersnapper. Get out of my way before you regret it.' The brute roared.

At this precise moment, Mother got out of the car. She called out not to me, but to Mags, who appeared to have shrunk in stature and struck dumb at the same time. She stepped between Mags' father and me; all five-foot-three of her.

'Magenta. Magenta, come to me, my sweetheart. Move away from that despicable man. I am your friend; please trust me.' Called Mother.

Mags did not move. The expression on her face was of pure terror. I felt so helpless, words alone would not diffuse this situation and I had no idea what the trigger had been for her father to treat Mags in such a brutal manner. The anxiety of the situation triggered the uncontrollable tics that I still suffered from at times of stress. My head was shaking and my eyelids were batting up and down. My left leg developed a life of its own as it shook, tapping my foot on the hardwood floor like a hysterical tap dancer.

On impulse, I decided that the only threat I could use was my intelligence. With a firm, steady voice I said 'that this day, along with my Mother, we had witnessed an act of domestic violence. As such, I felt inclined to report such an incident to the local authorities and the police, as I was concerned for Mags' safety.'

The words tumbled out of my mouth as though I had read them directly from a script. Somewhere, in the far reaches of my mind from some police drama or other, my brain had absorbed that prolific statement.

Mags' father's face was a sight to behold. He backed down like a scolded man. I wasn't expecting that. Since my unfortunate episode at primary school, when I defended my friend Philip, Mother taught me to use my words as weapons whenever possible. Today it had worked splendidly. He released his hold on Mags. Without looking at me, she ran like a scolded cat, into the house, followed closely by her father, as he slammed the door in my face. Mother put a reassuring arm on my shoulder.

'Come on, Alfie. There isn't anything else that we can do here today. However, tomorrow is another day and I see a girl who desperately needs our help and support. We will work something out together.'

We drove home in silence. I felt wired up, my tics refused to abate and my mind went up a gear. Truthfully, I was getting more anxious by the second as I fought to catch my breath that was trying to keep pace with my racing heart. Panic set in when my fingers and toes began to tingle. The pins and needles rendering my arms numb. Mother pulled the car over to the side of the road, opened the car windows and told me to breathe in and out at the same rate as herself. She held my hands between her own.

'Breathe Alfie, breathe. Follow my lead,' she kept repeating. She emphasised the rhythm of her own inhalation and slow expiration. At first, nothing changed, then gradually my chest and abdomen stopped rising and falling in great heaves until my breathing was in tune with Mother's. The whole episode had brought me out in a cold sweat, my forehead was dripping. I could taste the saltiness as it dripped onto my top lip. The adrenaline was surging through my body, with nowhere to go. I had no choice other than allowing the whole chemical process to stabilise as nature intended.

Leaving the car windows open, we continued on our way home in relative silence. Each with our own thoughts about the impact of the situation we had witnessed, which was breaking my heart into tiny, painful fragments of despair.

CHAPTER TWENTY-SIX

Grace's Diary

DECEMBER 1995

I am concerned about Alfie's friend Magenta. Over the last year, they have become very close. I think they are just good friends. Although, I suspect Alfie hopes for more than friendship, which is to be expected at his age. Alfie has never had a girlfriend before, to my knowledge. In fact, I don't think he has had any interest in girls before. I have always known that he is not like other boys.

Perhaps it may have helped if Paul had told him about his own experiences as a teenager and how to avoid peer pressure from classmates. I guess he must have experienced some of his own difficulties at school. Learning the hard way how to deal with the situations that can arise in a young man's life, especially when it comes to relationships with girls. The thing is, I don't want Alfie to see me as meddling in his social life. It is difficult for any parent to stand by and watch their child deal with the slings and arrows of teenage years.

I see how affectionate he is towards Magenta. I also see that she is holding herself back for whatever reason. Of course, that can be a sensible attitude. After all, they are young and have great expectations in terms of their individual futures. My problem with all this is Alfie's vulnerability in terms of his emotions.

As a parent, it is painful to stand by and watch your child suffer unrequited love and in Alfie's case even more so because he is not emotionally strong. When, on the odd occasion he forms a bond with someone, it is usually so profound for him that the other person feels overwhelmed. Generally, they make their excuses and drift away. Alfie understands why and knows that most people find him difficult to associate with because of his intense attitude and his anxieties.

Magenta is not like any other girl I have come across. In some ways, she reminds me of Alfie in terms of being different. I don't just mean about the way she dresses and her interest in Paganism, which I guess is just a teenage phase. No, it goes much deeper than that. She is like a female version of Alfie without the tics. Although I doubt if she sees herself like that.

Magenta very rarely talks about herself or her family. Most of her conversations with me are around my work. Since my promotion as a dietetic advisor for the school healthy eating programme, I have been able to use the skills and knowledge gained from my studies, to benefit the growth and development of the children who stay for school dinners. The Social Science teacher has invited me to give a presentation to the fourth-year students. I am a little worried, but very flattered. When I told Magenta, she was most interested. In fact, she appears to admire me.

Once, I asked about the type of food her mum likes to cook. She said that her mother wasn't fond of cooking, baking, or anything else come to think of it. She hinted that there was someone else who took care of the housekeeping. Perhaps her mum works full-time and her grandmother lives with them and takes cares of the house. I have noticed that Magenta usually tries hard not to talk about her family, she always changes the topic if they are brought up. Perhaps she is ashamed or embarrassed about them?

3 JANUARY 1996

We had a busy Christmas this year. Alfie had to work quite a few shifts at the restaurant, so I invited Pam and Hazel round for some girls' nights. I talked to them about my concerns over Alfie and how I think he is falling in love with Magenta. They are not keen on her because she is a goth. Sometimes I am ashamed of how narrow-minded people can be.

Pam said that she was relieved to hear that he was interested in girls. Everyone in the family was happy that he seemed to be turning out more *normal* than expected. This made me angry. I think Mum, Dad, and Pam are always gossiping about Alfie and questioning my parenting.

Hazel said that if Alfie has a girlfriend then surely, I should move on and find myself a new man.

Mum, Dad, and Pam gave me a Clinique make-up set for Christmas with a rather bright red lipstick in it. Pam and Hazel gave me a makeover with it. Well, I looked ridiculous. I felt like a clown. They don't understand that I like being natural and I have no desire to tart myself up. Perhaps I should ask Magenta to give me a makeover next. I wonder how everyone would react if I went out with thick black eyeliner and black lipstick.

17 FEBRUARY 1996

It's been an eventful Valentines weekend. Alfie came home with Magenta after work on Sunday and she looked very anxious and upset. At first, I wondered if Alfie had made a mistake. He told me he wanted to buy her a Valentine's gift and I wondered if he had purchased her something inappropriate. Perhaps I should have helped him.

However, I later found out it wasn't that. She didn't eat much food and then allowed me to drive her home. She appeared frightened and on edge. This is the first time she has ever allowed me to do this, which I found very surprising and a little unsettling, especially considering the unusual mood that Magenta was in.

I drove her home and was shocked to find out that she lives in an exclusive new housing development. It's well out of my league in terms of house prices – they must have money. I think she played down this side of her life so as to not intimidate Alfie. After all, she is a very gentle and kind soul who frequently speaks of helping less fortunate people. She may have found it difficult to admit to Alfie that she was from a privileged background.

They may have money, but her father is the most despicable man I have ever met. When I dropped her off it was horrendous. There is something not right in their home. The way Magenta's father treated her was so horrendous. I found it hard to believe a man who appears to have made a living successful enough to afford a luxury home could behave the way of a low life thug. He dragged her into the house as though she was a rag doll. She looked so afraid. I wanted to intervene, but that man is a beast of the very worst kind. Thank goodness Alfie never went there alone. I am so grateful they spent their time together at my house.

9 MARCH 1996

Alfie is still extremely traumatised by what happened at Magenta's house. His anxiety and tics have worsened. At times, I wonder whether he has developed epilepsy, such is the extent of his body movements. He can't sleep. Every night I hear him pacing up and down his bedroom. This situation cannot go on, he will become sleep deprived and I worry so much it will have an impact on his mental health.

I won't talk to him about Magenta until I feel that he is more stable. If Alfie allows the bad thoughts to crowd his mind, they will overwhelm him and drive him to despair.

We have not had any contact from Magenta or her family. Not that I expect to hear from her father. However, there was a remote possibility that Magenta or her mother, might have made contact if only to chat about her daughter's friendship with my son.

Alfie was not in any fit state to attend school for the week after the incident. I am worried as this has caused him to be a week behind with his work, adding extra pressure. By Friday evening, Alfie was more or less back to himself, his tics had settled to a more manageable and tolerable level. He has kept himself busy with his studies and I feel content that he is moving on. He has spent a long time tidying his bedroom and has organised all of his videos and books in alphabetical order. He is trying to keep his mind busy.

Alfie finally opened up to me and started talking about Magenta. He said that he had been worried about Magenta for some time. Alfie surprised me and said that a while ago, he noticed bruising on her wrists and upper arms. Apparently, she wears long sleeved tops and long black skirts to cover them up. He also told me how Mags removes her make-up and piercings before going home. I hear alarm bells at the mention of bruising. I need to get to the bottom of this, as something sinister is going on.

I asked Alfie some very personal questions about his sexual relationship with Magenta. He said that Magenta never flirted with him or led him to believe that she wanted more than a cuddle or to hold hands. He told me that they had kissed, but not French kissed like in the movies. I didn't realise he paid attention to those rom-coms I sometimes watch.

What he said next surprised me even more, he said that 'he wished that Magenta longed for him, like he does her. He said he loved her and was desperate to see her again.'

His words struck an uneasy pain in my heart, while my over imaginative mind tossed all kinds of unhealthy thoughts around. Thoughts I could not even begin to discuss with Alfie. I asked him if he felt well enough to go to work as usual on Saturday evening, to which he replied that wild horses would not keep him away.

I want to help Magenta. I have grown extremely fond of her and can't bear to think that she may be suffering in some way. There must be something that Alfie and I can do. Without any doubt, I am going to investigate all of this further. I want my boy to be happy, she is his first love. Paul was my first love and I was his. I hope this can be resolved. My heart goes out to Alfie.

CHAPTER TWENTY-SEVEN

Alfie

I t's been a tough week by all accounts, every second of the day has felt like an eternity. Saturday could not arrive soon enough for me. It is with sadness and a degree of trepidation that I arrive at work for my shift as a waiter, a job I thoroughly enjoy, made all the more pleasant by the fact that Mags and I work so well together.

We are known amongst the staff as the best tag team ever. I guess that Mags and I have such good chemistry that we bounce off one another, much like molecules and kinetic energy. Tonight, I arrive super early in anticipation of catching Mags before we start. The whole team gradually arrive, with the exception of Mags.

We usually have a ten-minute meeting before we start, so that we are made aware of any changes to the menu and how many available tables are free for customers who may drop by. We are introduced to a new waiter by the name of Andrew. Then the bombshell is dropped. He is to replace my beloved Mags who apparently has given in her notice to leave. To say that I am upset is an understatement, the truth is I am truly devastated. My mind begins to feel out of control and obsessive thoughts reverberate around and around. A tangle of negative feelings creeps through my body like vines wrapping around me, getting tighter and tighter until I almost feel choked.

I excuse myself from the rest of the team and make my way to the restroom, where I lean against the washbasin and take deep, slow breaths until I begin to feel in control. After splashing my face with cold water and putting on a brave face, I somehow, against all odds, manage to fulfil my role as a waiter. I guess for the most part I was working in a daze, managing most of my tasks by memory, for I felt spaced out and strangely numb. I found it exhausting trying to separate my thoughts and feelings.

When my shift is over I knock-on Mr Rossi's door and get called in. It is only the second time that I have entered this room, on my first day of employment and this time it was to give my notice of intention to leave.

When asked for the reason I was leaving I was honest with my reply. I explained that I could no longer work there now that Mags had left. Especially as she had not indicated to me that was her intention.

I was taken back when informed that Mags had not made contact with respect to leaving her job. It had, in fact, been her father who had given notice on her behalf. Mr Rossi seemed unusually perturbed. He spoke to me about his years of experience in the restaurant business and of the many people he had met and he wasn't impressed with the current situation.

'Between you and me, Alfie,' he said. 'I didn't like the tone of his voice, he was extremely aggressive and obnoxious. Horrible man. I've always had a soft spot for Magenta and you come to that. You will both be greatly missed by me and the team. Good luck with your studies lad. You might be a bit different to most young men of your age, but you have a good brain that will help to carry you through any future difficulties. Go get your girl and look after her.'

When Mother came to pick me up from work, I informed her that was my last shift at Antico's and I would be looking for a new job. She did not seem surprised when I told her that Mags had also given notice, or rather, her father had done it for her.

We didn't go straight home, instead, Mother took a detour that took us past Mags' house. It was in darkness except for two outside lights. There was a large saloon car parked on the drive and a child's bike was laid on its side, strewn across the lawn.

Mother slowed the car right down as we approached the house. For a moment, I thought she was going to stop, get out and go to the door there and then. I wondered if Mother had turned into Cagney or Lacy, but no, she just checked the house over and drove home.

On Sunday mornings we usually relax in our sleepwear. We drink coffee and read the newspapers, which Mother has delivered. Generally, we discuss the state of the nation, laugh about the gossip columns and look at the sports pages. However, this time other plans are afoot. This becomes apparent when Mother enters the lounge dressed very formally with full make-up and a serious expression on her face.

'Ok Alfie, today is the day. Go and have a shower. Put on some clean jeans and a decent shirt. No goth clothes today, please. I will have breakfast ready for you and then we are going to meet Magenta's family.'

So, my Mother really had turned into a detective and I was very proud of her indeed. Determined to get the show on the road, I quickly showered and changed into what I considered to be a most suitable outfit. I splashed some Brut aftershave on that Father had given me for Christmas and I was good to go.

I found my best Nike trainers, gave them a spray of deodorant to freshen them up and entered the kitchen to be greeted with the sound of sausages sizzling in a frying pan. She had made me my favourite sausage sandwich with one side of the bread toasted. I wolfed it down as Mother stood by watching.

'It's good to see you haven't lost your appetite son, considering the recent events. Are you alright? About this, I mean, are you ok for me to visit Magenta in her own home? Perhaps we should take something with us as an excuse for visiting, any ideas?'

I thought about this for a moment and remembered the psychology book that Mags had encouraged me to read. She was keen for me to read about Freud's ideas in relation to mental health problems and psychosis. The book belonged to Mags which she had made quite clear with her name written on the inside cover.

Book in hand, we approached the front door which only one week ago had been slammed rudely in my face. Having pressed the doorbell, we patiently waited for a response. We waited and waited, until Mother could stand it no more, then she rattled the door knocker loud enough to waken the dead. That got a response. The door was opened slowly, revealing a frail woman, of an age, I wouldn't like to guess. Her features were choleric in nature and her hair looked as though it may have been dark at some stage but was currently salt and pepper. A forelock of hair was covering one of her eyes and she constantly tried to discipline it into place with a thin veined hand. This woman could not be Mags' mum. How wrong was I?

Mother was the first to speak, enquiring if Magenta was at home. The lady looked puzzled at the mention of Mags' name and I thought that perhaps she was hard of hearing. The moment was broken as a young girl of around eight years of age, came to the door. She resembled Mags so much that she took my breath away.

'Hello,' I said, 'you must be Magenta's sister?'

To which she smiled and told me that she only had two sisters, Vanessa and Sissy. Meanwhile, the lady had somehow regained her hearing.

'You must be Vanessa's friend young man. Are you Alfie?'

Now I was totally confused and so was Mother. She inquired if perhaps we could talk in the house rather than standing on the doorstep. Reluctantly, she allowed us through the door. The young girl skipped ahead of us, calling for Vanessa.

We were directed to the left of the hallway and entered a large lounge area, double the size of our own front room. Mother remained standing, she turned to the lady who had directed us to the lounge and asked if she was a relative of Magenta. Perhaps Mother was speaking in a foreign language or maybe her accent was difficult for this strange woman, because no answer was given in reply. She just stared at my Mother with a quizzical look on her face.

A sudden commotion distracted me as Magenta limped nervously into the lounge area. She was dragging her left foot and appeared to be in some discomfort. She increased her step as she made her way towards me, never taking her eyes off me for a second. As Mags got closer, I noticed the bruising around her puffy eyes and her swollen upper lip. I ran towards my Mags, hugging her gently for fear of causing her harm. She had lost even more weight and I could feel her ribs beneath my touch. She whispered into my right ear.

'Call me Vanessa for that is my birth name. Magenta is my goth name. I keep my two lives separate as a means of survival.'

Well, I wasn't expecting that. My Mags had given herself a totally separate identity away from home. In terms of her goth appearance I was aware of that, but a new name. It was as if she was denying her own identity or perhaps hiding behind a new one. Whatever the reason, I had the distinct feeling that it was a defence mechanism. She mentioned survival, to me this suggested she was in danger and I had a good idea who the likely perpetrator was.

Her mother just stood there, as though in some kind of trance or drugged stupor, constantly shifting her body weight on one leg, then the other. That annoying forelock of hair was repeatedly flopping over her tired looking eyes; she looked like a lost soul.

I guess she must have recently lost weight for her clothes were hanging off her, as though they had once belonged to someone with a fuller figure. The clothes looked to be of good quality, but were very outdated compared to the type of style my Mother wore. Another thing that struck me about her was her hands, which were thin and bony, her nails chewed down, practically to the flesh. On her third-finger, on her left-hand, she had the biggest diamond ring I had ever laid eyes on. It looked like it was about to drop off her skinny finger. As if she had read my thoughts, she nervously pushed the ring further down her finger. I guess someone must have loved her very much at some time to have given her such a huge rock.

Mags continued to stay close by my side, she put a finger to her lips and said shush while she motioned for Mother and me to follow her. We quietly followed Mags through the lounge and into a conservatory that overlooked a huge lawn with borders of plants and flowers. Not like the ones we have at home. These were set out like a stately home, all meticulously planned and colour coordinated. Her mother followed us at a snail's pace, always a few steps behind us. It was as if she was a servant and a dutiful one at that.

Mother's expression was giving nothing away. Despite the obvious bruising to Mags face. I could tell that she was taking in the surroundings much like myself, but showed no sign of surprise, in fact, if anything she behaved nonchalant even unimpressed.

Mags suggested we sit down so that we could explain the purpose of our visit. I think this was a smoke screen. She knew exactly why we had come and she was playing for time. Probably hoping her mother would leave us alone. Then I remembered the book that I was clutching in my hand.

'Vanessa, I thought you might need this. You left it at work,' I lied. 'And being as you have given in your notice, me too by the way, I thought I'd save you a journey and bring it to you.'

Mags smiled a crooked, painful smile. She was grateful that I had not mentioned that the book was in fact left at my house. Her mother seemed satisfied with the reason for our visit. In fact, if I were to correctly read the expression on her face, I could see a shadow of relief pass across it.

Mags gently asked her mother if perhaps she could make some tea for the guests as they had been kind enough to return her psychology book.

Well done Mags. Her mother left us alone, I guess it would take some time for the tea to appear if it took her as long to make the tea as it did to answer the door. The moment she was out of earshot, Mother left her chair and went over to Mags. No words were spoken at first, just a gentle hug and a reassuring stroke of her cheek. Tears began to trickle down Mags' face, slowly and quietly at first until I held her hand, which triggered such raw emotion as I have ever witnessed. Between the sobbing, she repeatedly asked for our help. Mother tried to coax Mags to explain the reasons for this, but the only clue that she gave us was that she couldn't help her sister. She repeated this a number of times and then she looked at me with such a painful expression that my heart began to race and make me catch my breath.

'Please Mags, please,' I begged. 'Let us help. Come home with us, you will be safe. Whatever is upsetting you is related to this house and I have a good idea that it is that brute of a man, who behaves like no father that I know.'

'You don't understand, Alfie,' she sobbed. 'No one can help me or my sisters. Mum is always unwell and weak-minded; he has driven her to madness. She used to be a strong, wonderful mum. Now, she can't go anywhere. Everything Mum does is strictly timed and monitored. He deliberately returns home at random times to check on her, to make sure she has not gone anywhere. She has no friends now, he made sure of that. He tells her what clothes to wear, he has ruined her and is set on ruining me and my sisters. I could not prevent him from hurting me and now he is hurting Sissy.'

A flurry of images surge through my mind, memories of the day I first encountered that belligerent man who does not deserve to be a father. Mother was out of her depths, I could see that, and Mags' mother was likely to return any minute. I needed to know how exactly her father was hurting her.

The truth is, when the answer came I was not prepared for such a shocking disclosure of sexual abuse that Mags had been submitted to since the age of nine. Now her sister, Sissy, had become another victim of her father's depravity.

We were shocked beyond belief. I did the first thing that came to mind and I lifted Mags from the sofa, cradled her in my arms and told her that I was taking her home with me.

Mother rushed ahead of me, opening doors until we were outside. As Mother pulled off the drive, the car wheels skidded and screeched. Through the rear-view window, I saw Mags' mother at the front door and I swear that she had a smile on her face. Was it a smile? Or was it relief that her daughter would now be safe and that her husband would get exactly what he deserved?

We didn't go home. Instead, Mother drove to the police station. Whilst I comforted Mags in the back of the car, Mother went to the desk clerk and reported that despicable man.

A female police officer came out of the station and asked Magenta if she was willing to go with her for a chat.

Mags gently nodded her head. She looked so small and vulnerable. My heart ached at the sight of her being supported around the waist. Almost trance-like, she limped through the huge oak door leading into the police station. As she was led away, Mags turned her face towards me and Mother, she gave us a painful smile followed by a gentle nod of her head.

Mother and I were offered a drink, which we gratefully accepted. We were then ushered into separate interview rooms and asked to write a statement of an account of the events as we had witnessed, leading up to the current time. Despite the overwhelming emotion, which had once again triggered my tics into uncontrollable body movements, I agreed to write a statement.

The young police officer could not help but notice the involuntary movements of my body and kindly asked if I was willing to be seen and examined by the on-call doctor.

It had been years since my initial assessment at the child psychology unit and I considered the offer for a moment. I came to the conclusion that a medical examination within a police station would probably not look good on my medical records, should they need to be checked in the future, for occupational purposes. With this in mind, I declined, but I was grateful for the offer. Concentrating on my breathing helped to relax me enough to think clearly about the events that had led up to this moment.

With hindsight, I now realised that Mags' behaviour had always been defensive. She had never spoken of her parents with any affection and had appeared overly concerned about her sisters, who were now clearly the objects of her father's twisted, pervasive sexual desires, as he was now abusing them instead of Mags.

I wrote my statement; outlining how she had altered not only her appearance, but her birth name, which I had only just discovered was Vanessa, not Magenta as she preferred to be called. I guess on her employment application she must have put her real name for the documentation and requested to be called Magenta.

It occurred to me that her father had likely been sexually abusing, manipulating and controlling Mags since childhood and on reaching her teens she has somehow, against all odds, found the strength and determination to fight back. Although she had tried to find some happiness by creating a new identity away from home, the situation must have been emotionally exhausting. I guess her father knew that he was losing coercive control over Mags and had switched his attention to her younger sisters, for which Mags must have felt responsible, knowing that he had started abusing them as he had done to her. I could not get my head around this at all, especially as he apparently portrayed himself as a good Catholic husband and father. What a hypocrite. How could he possibly consider himself a Christian?

My own parents had never forced any kind of religious belief on to me. Personally, I don't believe that in order to be a good Christian, one has to go to a building with an altar, all man-made and pray to a God who we can only read about in stories, much like any other fairy tale. In my mind, a good person proves themselves by being honest, kind and good. The Ten Commandments are an excellent set of guidelines that have stood the test of time, something that Mags' father conveniently overlooked.

I wrote about the bruises I had seen on her wrists and arms and how she always wore either long skirts or trousers and long sleeves. The first encounter with her father and the abusive manner in which he treated her I reported in great detail, hopefully, word for word the dialogue that passed between us. Finally, as difficult as it was, I wrote down the painful conversation that had prompted me to save my Mags and hopefully her sisters, from any further physical and psychological pain at the hands of their father. I signed the statement as requested and was directed to the reception area, where Mother was waiting.

Mags was nowhere to be seen, so I enquired at the desk as to when she could join us.

The desk sergeant shook his head and told me that 'Vanessa was to await the social services assessment and it was likely that she would not be returning home, at least not that night, until a full investigation had taken place.'

We reluctantly left the police station and silently made our way home. Exactly one week after our encounter with the police, we had a visit from a family liaison officer who came to offer support and a referral for counselling to help us come to terms with any unresolved emotions surrounding the situation we had encountered.

Although reluctant to discuss the case, she informed us that Mags and her sisters were in temporary foster care and her mother had been admitted to the local psychiatric unit as she had reached crisis point when she witnessed the arrest of her husband.

The young officer was extremely kind and helpful. She spoke to us about the benefit of talking therapy and of sharing any distressing thoughts and feelings that may manifest in the mind resulting in potential depression. I don't think either Mother or I were well placed to make a decision that day. I guess she realised this and left us her contact details for future reference. Try as I might, no one was willing to give me a contact number for Mags, I had no idea where she was.

Most days after school I hung around outside her school gates on the off chance that she had continued her education there. One day, in desperation, I called into the school secretary and was informed that Mags no longer attended. I was devastated. There was a huge empty hole inside of my heart that was filled with a pain impossible to describe.

The pain was further reinforced when Mother drove me past her house and a sold sign was swinging on a post outside. This felt like the beginning of the end for me. The end of all hope, that Mags, her mother and sisters may return to the family home and pick up the pieces of their fractured lives. These repeated daily lashings of stress are tearing me apart and I am too proud and private to tell anyone the extent of my suffering, sometimes the loneliest place in the world is slap bang in the middle of a crowd, this is how I feel. The inability to communicate my feelings is building up inside of me, the pressure is unbearable.

That day marked the starting point of the destructive self-harm I began to inflict upon myself. At first, I began to pull out my eyelashes, one at a time. Each tiny sting of pain released the tension that was building behind my eyes. This way I managed to momentarily bring myself back to some kind of reality as I sat at my desk working on the all-important assignments that were part of my A-level studies. At first, the odd missing eyelash was barely noticeable, but within a few weeks, I was devoid of any protective hair to my eyes, as I had managed successfully to pull out every last lash, top and bottom.

By this point, Mother had noticed. Mainly due to the fact that the rims of my eyes looked red and my usually big brown eyes somehow looked lost and sunken within in my face. Her concern touched me deeply, but lying came easily to me, especially when in my own defence, so I tried to persuade her that it was due to the constant rubbing of my eyes as a result of the strain of my constant studying. To be fair, I don't think she was altogether convinced, but it gave me breathing space.

After school, I spent the majority of time studying for my upcoming mock A-level exams. This appeared to keep Mother happy. I know she purposely did not bring up the subject of Magenta in order to spare my feelings, however, she could not protect me from myself and the constant torment of my overactive mind. I was experiencing unwanted sexual images twenty-four hours a day of Mags and her sisters being abused by her father. I was finding it sick and terrifying. My reality checks and release came with self-harm. I slowly progressed from my eyelashes to my hair, discreetly pulling out individual hairs from various points on my scalp. In the privacy of my bedroom, I systematically pulled out every pubic hair I possessed, leaving raised, red, irritating spots, like tombstones, marking the area where they once belonged. Keeping this destructive behaviour secretive was draining every calorie of energy from me and although I was eating well, my weight declined with the risk of becoming noticeable by others. To avoid worrying Mother, I began to layer my clothes, to pack out my skinny frame, however, it was difficult to disguise the weight-loss from my face and the thinning of my hair as a result of me pulling it out. I reached crisis point on the day I read a report on the front page of our local newspaper. The headlines caught my eye as I read, 'Local Paedophile's Wife Commits Suicide Before his Trial.'

That very same day I cut myself for the first time. Using a sharp blade, I drew a line down the inside of my left forearm and watched the blood drip onto the carpet. Mother caught me in the act. The horrified look on her face caused me to break down in front of her and confess my intrusive thoughts and the sick, unwanted images that I had been experiencing during the months since I had lost my precious Mags.

CHAPTER TWENTY-EIGHT

Grace's Diary

21 APRIL 1996

I am losing my boy, my sweet Alfie. I can't cope. I can't sleep. I am scared that I am going to lose him forever. Ever since he read the newspaper report about Magenta's family, he has taken his self-harming to a new level. In addition to pulling out his hair, he has started to cut himself. I was in shock when I saw blood running down his arm. How can he do that to himself? What is he thinking? How can I help him?

That beast of a man has ruined far too many lives, he is sick and needs locking away forever. Those poor girls ... I dread to think of the psychological trauma they have been through.

Alfie refuses to talk to me about the whole ordeal, he has locked it away somewhere in the corner of his heart and mind. He is stuck in his own private hell. I think the torment has grown so much that he is no longer able to contain it. Perhaps that is why he is self-harming. He is unable to put his feelings into words, only actions. I thought that I had raised Alfie to feel able to talk to me about anything. How could I have got this so wrong? Evidently, he has been harbouring sad thoughts and feels unable to speak about how he is suffering. He needs help. But if I can't bring him out of this darkness, who can?

I feel that I have let him down. Since the moment Alfie was born, he has been the centre of my universe, the sun in the centre of my own personal space. My first thought on waking and my last thought before sleeping. His welfare and in particular, his mental health and stability, have been my number one priority. A healthy mind and healthy body. I realise, of course, that he does not need me to be hovering over him 24/7. I have tried hard to keep my distance, watching over him, ready and willing to sacrifice whatever is needed. I will do anything it takes to help my son. Anything.

MAY 1996

I have organised for Alfie to have professional counselling to help him with his mental health problems. I feel that we can move forward. He has already had to deal with being different from his peer group and now his mental health has taken a severe battering. I only hope that this counsellor can help him. The doctor has suggested strong medication to help him. He seems far too young to be drugged up on anti-depressants.

My parents keep telling me that Alfie needs a strong father figure at home, however, I am not interested in anyone. They have been pestering me for years to start dating. I have deliberately avoided doing so as I didn't want any personal relationship with others to affect my relationship with my son. Many years ago, Alfie once encouraged me to remarry, which surprised me. Sometimes I feel lonely, a deep painful loneliness, especially at night time. I still miss Paul.

I shouldn't think of my own loneliness when my son is going through hell. I need to be strong for him. I need to help him. His whole future depends on finishing his education now and becoming mentally stable. That is my focus. His mental health, his happiness. My time will come when he is settled as a man.

I have saved up some money and I am thinking that perhaps Alfie and I need a change of scenery. I will ask Hazel to pick me up some brochures from the Co-op travel shop. A holiday might just be what Alfie needs.

JUNE 1995

After a lot of deliberation, I have found a package holiday, within budget. I'm very excited and plan to try as many Spanish food dishes as possible. Although money is tight, I have managed to buy myself a new swimming costume and a couple of sundresses. Pam has kindly lent me one of her fancy sarongs. My mum has also been generous and lent me her favourite sunhat. However, it looks a bit battered and well worn, which is not surprising, considering how many times she has squashed it into her suitcase. Father offered to lend Alfie his Panama hat, bless him. Alfie politely refused, explaining that he prefers a baseball hat. I guess he will be spending most of his time on the beach, so he will also be needing a few new pairs of shorts and a couple of tee-shirts. I think he has a few decent tops for the evening, even if they are a bit gothic looking.

I have been to the library and loaned a couple of Spanish language tapes. Alfie is a quick learner. Hopefully, between us, we will learn a few words to get us by. Costa Brava, here we come!

CHAPTER TWENTY-NINE

Alfie

I need some peace; my mind feels overwhelmed with unwelcome thoughts spinning around inside of my head colliding and crashing into each other. At times, I feel as though I am watching two movies at the same time. Currently, one side of my mind is buzzing with physics and equations. While on the other side, I am visualising sexuality, blasphemy, and violent acts. I want it to stop. I need peace and I need sleep as this exhaustion is driving me to despair. I need help.

Willingly, I attended the first of many sessions with the counsellor who reassured me that eventually, I would free my mind of the thoughts that constantly tortured me. My counsellor, Jan, was a very mature and a motherly type of woman who I felt immediately at ease with. She had a natural gift for teasing out the torturing thoughts that threatened to poison my mind. At times, during the consultations with Jan, I felt that if she scratched the surface of my skin, she could reach the pain beneath.

She asked me some very searching questions, covering subjects such as self-harm and if I had ever felt suicidal. She taught me how to bring hidden issues to the surface where I could talk them through and deal with them. Over a period of twelve weeks, although I didn't completely free my mind, I managed to move the thoughts into another compartment in my brain, put a padlock on them and throw away the key.

My education continued as a matter of course, almost as though I was on a pre-destined pathway on auto-pilot. When my A-level exams were completed, Father took me to his local pub for a pint with his mates. Mother had an altogether different plan, we flew to Spain, then caught a coach to a small resort on the Costa Brava called Tossa del Mar. I know Mother needed this break as much as I did, for she was not looking well at all and although she never complained. I knew she was having problems with her kidneys and frequently needed antibiotics to help fight the infection.

Watching the other families on the beach, playing together made me sad in some respects. Although Rose, my half-sister, is a great girl, our age difference makes it difficult at present to do things together. Maybe that will change in the future and perhaps Father may take me on holiday with them. For now, I watch other families messing about, playing football and frisbee.

Mother looks so exhausted, laying on the sun lounger, so I think it's best that I don't disturb her. I notice that some of the locals are setting up a volleyball net across the beach, close to where we are relaxing. I watch with interest and one of the guy's notices me watching.

He calls me over and in broken English asks me to join them.

I agree and for the rest of the week, on a daily basis, I enjoy playing volleyball with the Spanish guys. After the game, we all go in the pool and play water polo; these guys are fit. Mother is happy laying on the sun lounger, under a parasol, reading and snoozing.

Playing sport helps to free my mind, the invasive thoughts that sporadically emerge are kept at bay. I allow myself to reminisce, to remember the good times I shared with Magenta and the enlightenment I gained from our in-depth, philosophical conversations. In hindsight, I now understand why her views on religion were so different from my own. Her parents hid behind their so-called Catholic beliefs. How was it possible for a mother to stand by and witness the actions of her husband who pretended to be a good Catholic husband and father? What a bastard!

On the last day of our holiday, I am invited out with the team to the local tapas bar. We eat the most delicious tapas and drink the local beer. I have managed to pick up a few Spanish words and phrases and somehow between us, we have a conversation around the usual 'male' topics of football, girls, and the latest music. The night ends with a lot of backslapping and handshakes with a promise to return again one day in the future. Nice thought, but I guess these type of promises, are unlikely to materialise.

On our flight home, worry gradually seeps its way into my over-active mind. My A-level results will be arriving at school next week. Although I have a good idea what my grades will be, there is always the possibility that they will not be good enough, for my preferred first choice of university. I have been offered a place at three universities to study pharmacology. Truth be known that in a heartbeat, I would choose any one of them if I knew that Mags was going to be there. I have no idea how to make contact with her. I know that she wanted to study law and her predicted grades would suggest that she had a good chance of a university offer, but considering everything that had happened to her, I can't help thinking that perhaps she may have lost sight of her dreams. I hope not. Mags has such potential and her understanding of psychology is quite remarkable.

Mother seems to think that the social services would have made every possible attempt to place Mags and her sisters together with a member of her extended family. If not, then a temporary foster family until further arrangements could be made. I know she would assist the authorities in every way possible to keep the family together. They had been through so much. I can't even begin to imagine how I would feel if Mother died, even worse under the circumstances of suicide.

Mags and her sisters will need lots of counselling and support. Her mother must have been so deeply entrenched with guilt and remorse knowing what her husband was doing to their daughters, that she felt suicide was the only way out. The more I turn these thoughts over in my head, the tighter my fists curl into themselves. I clench so tight that I feel my nails breaking the skin. When I open them, small moon shape cuts are emblazoned into my skin, red and angry, but it feels good. The pain feels good.

When my mind goes into overdrive like this, I can't seem to find my way back. My mind shifts from one crazy thought to another. I have a movie on a spool playing over and over again. The first part of the movie I see visions of Kenny, smiling at me while he is taking that fatal overdose. He looks happy as he sticks that damn hypodermic needle into his vein, then he reaches out to me, asking for help. Superimposed upon this vision is Mags, she is also smiling at me, then she raises her sleeves exposing multiple bruises on her pale skin. I feel that I am sliding into that deep pit of despair again, I desperately attempt to remember the counsellors' words of encouragement. She encouraged me to bring hidden issues to the surface where I can talk them through and deal with them before they poison my mind.

When my tics become noticeable, Mother reaches over and gently squeezes my hand.

'Are you alright Alfie, is something bothering you? Do you wish to talk about it?'

I shake my head and lie. Mother would never be able to comprehend the dreadful thoughts that run through my mind and I would not subject her to such horrors.

'Just thinking about my exam results, that's all,' I answer.

I was glad to get home to my own familiar bedroom, which I now viewed as my sanctuary. However, not for much longer, as I had agreed to spend the first year of my studies living in the halls of residence. I needed every help to be part of the group. I had deduced, that if I was offered a place at the University of Nottingham, even though I could probably commute, it would be in my best interests to be one of the lads living in halls. At least then, my chances of making friends would have a fighting chance. The thought of moving out, tormented me in one way and excited me in another.

Mother had already gathered a few essentials together on the chance of my grades being accepted. I told her it was tempting fate as my grades were not guaranteed, but she continued nonetheless.

In the far corner of my bedroom was a stack of packing boxes, containing towels, bedding and a variety of cooking utensils. Her recent purchase of an iron will unlikely get much use. I will be taking my stereo system and the small TV from my room along with my comfort blanket, a piece of Mother's old candlewick dressing gown. This will need to be well hidden from prying eyes. Very rarely do I think about it now, but when I was a child, just holding on to it, helped me to settle.

I needn't have worried as I was awarded A grades in all my subjects and an A-star in chemistry. My place at the University of Nottingham was secure. The next stage of my journey through life was there for me to grab and make the most of. However, though I was enthusiastic about the study and all that it entailed, my main concern was not about the learning and all of the hard graft, no, my brain was up for it but was my mind strong enough to carry me through? Somehow, I needed to find the strength to break free from my destructive, negative thoughts and let go of Mags. I knew she desperately wanted me to succeed, as I did for her. So, I must concentrate now on my future. My parents have such great hopes for me in terms of a career, especially Father, who is delighted that his son has broken the mould and won't be working down the mine like himself and his ancestors. Although he never grumbled about the conditions down on the coal face, the scars of his work are visible on his body in the form of blue stained scars, resembling miniature tattoos of discriminate shapes.

Of late, I noticed that his breathing is a little laboured and he is wheezy at times. Musical sounds can be quite clearly heard coming from his chest, especially when he exerts himself. It is common knowledge that the air quality down the mines is not conducive to good health. It is of poor quality, something the old miners can testify to. One only has to visit the local hospital respiratory ward to see the overwhelming number of ex-miners suffering from obstructive pulmonary disease or pneumoconiosis.

The air quality in the local Miner's Welfare Club can't be any better. There is always a fog of smoke in the main room, as a consequence of the multitude of smokers, all puffing away on their Park Drives and Senior Service. I can clearly remember Father smelling of stale tobacco smoke whenever he took me out on Sunday afternoons. His new wife also smells of nicotine, but mixed with the smell of stale perfume. She is so unlike Mother. I am very proud of the way Mother is her own person, has never felt the need to follow the sheep or wear the current fashions, no matter how absurd.

My Mother is smart in every way, not only in her dress sense, which is always impeccable, but also in her outlook and her beliefs. I know she will profoundly miss me when I go to university and yet she selflessly continues to encourage me with my plans to stay in halls for the first year. I know Mother has made sacrifices in terms of saving for my future. She has enough put by to cover my expenses for the next two years. With hard work on my part, I hope to contribute towards my final years of study. Time will tell. I know Mother has a fulfilling career and her working week is quite hectic, however, I can't help wondering how she is going to manage her weekends.

My grandparents are no longer able to travel to far off places. I expect she will fuss around them. Mother plans to cook Sunday lunch for them, that way she will have company at the dining table. Otherwise, it will be very lonely sat alone eating her home-cooked roast dinner.

I think their money ran out before their inclination to travel dwindled. Grandmother is around seventy-five now. I think Grandfather is probably around seventy-eight. Considering he also worked down the mine like my father, his lungs have not suffered to the same extent as most of the miners around these parts. Grandfather says it is because he never smoked or chewed tobacco.

That sounds gross to me. Apparently, in Grandfather's day, it was common practice to sniff something called snuff. I guess it wasn't as addictive as the upcoming practice amongst the rich and famous to sniff cocaine. He also declined the snuff. I think Grandmother was always keeping a watchful eye on him in his youth. It is hard to imagine my Grandfather being eighteen like me.

He once told me that he had been a good scholar and had very much enjoyed his school years. Much to my surprise, he had won a scholarship to attend the local grammar school, but his parents could not afford the uniform and the P.E. kit, not to mention the books.

He started working down the mines at the age of fourteen. No wonder he and Grandmother chose to travel when he retired, I guess it helped to compensate for his lost opportunities. When I was younger, I didn't really like my grandparents much, but now I see life from a different perspective, this is helping me to understand them more.

When I told them that I had been offered a place at the university, I swear that there were tears in my Grandfather's old, weary eyes. He smoothed the fine grey hair from his forehead and shook my hand.

'Alfie,' he said. 'You and I haven't always seen eye to eye. You are a strange lad with your obsessive ways and peculiar tics. Not to mention your dalliance with drink and drugs and yet you remind me of myself. You have a keen eye for detail and a great ability to remember facts and figures. I am so proud of you Alfie; we both are. Your mother has done a really good job raising you on her own. We know it hasn't been easy for her, she has also done us proud. We don't tell her often enough, I know.'

Grandmother gave me a hug and pressed an envelope into my hand.

'For you, Alfie we have kept a distant eye on you and our Grace. I know at times she felt that we were not supportive enough, stating we were gallivanting around Europe. Truth is, we needed to make the best of these last few years before old age took over and rendered us sick and immobile. Grandfather's health has been so much better than we anticipated. A long time ago we set a little something aside for you. Don't worry about your Mum, we will keep her busy,' she laughed.

The envelope contained a check for £200. There was a note inside, it was a written request to open a student bank account and to only use the money in an emergency. Grandmother's squiggly signature and Grandfather's amazing calligraphy signature completed the note.

We may be a working-class family and I assume I will be socialising with students from a variety of backgrounds, however, my roots I will hold close and the sacrifice and generosity of Mother and her parents will not be wasted. Although my parents were no longer married, they recognised the importance of pulling together when it mattered. We went as a family to the university campus. The car was full of suitcases and packing boxes, much the same as all of the other cars pulling into the car park. There were signs everywhere pointing to the different administration areas. My documentation pointed me in the direction of the central admin point, I had been allocated a reference number and joined a queue of equally excited students. The atmosphere was electric.

Whilst in the queue, I glanced around, taking note of the other students. Most of them looked to be roughly my age, although there was a scattering of more mature students. I noticed a large number of foreign looking students, some Chinese, others looked possibly eastern European, also a group of Spanish students. I know this because I recognised some of the words that I had picked up from the guys I had met on holiday. As always, there was one face in the crowd that I was searching for, but Mags were nowhere to be seen.

Eventually, I reached the front of the queue handed over my documentation and in return was passed the keys to my room and an even bigger pile of documents. Meanwhile, Mother and Father had been exploring the grounds, I met them as they were returning to the car. They both looked so relaxed together and not for the first time did I regret never telling Mother about the times I saw Father with the woman who stole him away. Perhaps our lives would have been so different, I may have had a brother to share my life with or even a sister as lovely as Rose.

Sometimes these thoughts and others turn around and round in my head, driving me crazy. It is as though they are in a loop or stuck in a groove, whining and whining inside of my mind. My thoughts are broken when Mother mentions food. We had all been so busy, we had lost track of time. They had found a Students' Union bar that sold hot dogs and burgers amongst other fast food delights. We made our way to the Students' Union bar, passing a number of older students handing out leaflets to join the Students' Union, promising to get a discount on a number of important items, not least alcoholic drinks.

All very tempting, I thought. The bar was buzzing with students and a few parents, who looked equally as ill at ease as my own. We ordered bacon cobs and coffee, eventually managing to locate a sticky table and some very uncomfortable chairs. Despite the rancid smell of cooking fat in the air, the bacon cobs were very good, the bread fresh and filled with a generous portion of bacon.

I took the opportunity to flip through some of the paperwork I had been handed with the keys. The directions to my dorm appeared easy to follow and by the time we had finished our coffee, I had a good idea of the direction we were to follow. We decided to walk to the dorm and check out the nearest car park. The bloke I was allocated appeared to be specifically for males, which made sense, I suppose, although I suspect it will be awash with female company before the week is out.

While Father went back to the car, Mother and I checked out my room. I was on the ground floor, which could be an advantage if returning back drunk and a disadvantage from the noise perspective, as I will hear all of the other students coming and going. My room was not quite as big as I was expecting, but it had the advantage of its own bathroom. There was a battered looking wooden desk with an old-fashioned angle pose lamp, set close to the window for maximum light. A hardwood chair that looked as though it had been rescued from an old Victorian school prior to demolition. A single bed with a bedside cabinet, a wardrobe and a very high chest of drawers. I half expected to see a list of rules pinned to the back of the door, signed by Mr Choakumchild, a teacher from the imaginations of Charles Dickens. Instead, there were just instructions related to fire safety.

The room needed a woman's touch to make it homelier, which is exactly what Mother did the moment Father put the packing boxes in the room. I had no idea of the assortment of items she had spirited away in the packing boxes. Out came the duvet and pillows, within minutes she had made up the bed and threw a load of patterned cushions against the wooden headboard. She put a table lamp on the bedside cabinet and a bright red wool rug on the floor next to the bed. Father set up the TV and my stereo system on top of the chest of drawers, while I unpacked my clothes and books. I set the books out in alphabetical order and lined up my pens in a neat line. The walls looked a bit bare. I guess I should have bought some of my posters from home. Not to worry; I can get some new ones, perhaps a few pin-up girls? Each floor of the dorms had a well-equipped kitchen and a common room, containing easy chairs and a coffee table and lots of ashtrays.

My parents left shortly after we had checked out the rest of the building, I waved them off with the promise to keep in touch. Father had given me a mobile phone and the promise of a pay as you go top-up card, which he would post to me every month, with a letter from himself or my sister Rose. I thought this was a real sensible gift from him and a guarantee that I was able to communicate with my family at all times.

In addition, he gave me £20 and told me to expect a cheque every month along with the top-up card. I was very touched. Father still has a family to support and yet he is prepared to financially support me. Mother has set up a regular allowance to be paid into my account to cover expenses including my accommodation. I know I have a lot to be grateful for, one day in the not too distant future, I hope to repay my family in one way or another. For now, I need to study pharmacology and tomorrow I will meet my fellow students.

The noise outside my room is quieting down, I should think that most of the students have settled into their respective rooms by now. While looking out of my window at the courtyard facing me, someone had slipped a note under the door. It was from the Students' Union inviting all the fresher's, I guess that must mean me, to an evening of fun and entertainment in the union bar. Well, that certainly sounds interesting and a good opportunity to meet some of the other students. I am not under any illusion, I guess the same old rules apply, the popular guys, the jocks will all gravitate towards one another, the nerds and the oddballs (that's me) will also find their place in the pecking order of university society. That's ok, I am comfortable with who I am. I know that I can be annoying and when I get stressed my tics make me look an idiot. But hey, the girls never have a problem with me. Thank goodness, I inherited some advantages such as being tall, slim, and dark-haired, just like Father.

I have packed some of my old goth clothes. Crazy, I know, but it gives me a connection to Mags and takes me back to a time when I was part of a group of people who understood me. Perhaps I should be true to myself, clothes can reflect who you are and how you perceive yourself. There is no point in me dressing up as a cool guy because clearly, I am not cool. Equally, I am not a rich, fashion-conscious kid with money to spare. With this in mind, I put on my black tee-shirt with a grey spider's web pattern on the front, a pair of black jeans and black leather boots with a high lace up front, almost like oversized Doc Martins. With no intentions of spending any more than a tenner, I lock my wallet up in the desk and slip the tenner in my pocket.

My dorm is not much distance from the union bar and I easily find my way there, having been earlier. I can hear the music well before I arrive. Students are sitting in groups around the outside of the building, empty bottles of beer and cider scattered around them. Some of the girls are already drunk, laying on the floor, out cold. The scene takes me back to the time I was arrested by the police and taken to my grandparents. I remember how ill I felt the next day. It is not a feeling I want to repeat in a hurry. Suddenly a very attractive girl wearing the tightest denim skirt I have ever seen staggers towards me smiling.

'Hey gorgeous,' she slurs. 'Do I know you from somewhere?'

Before I get the opportunity to answer, she lunges forward and promptly vomits on the front of my tee-shirt.

'Nice,' I say and I help her to her feet.

'Oh god, I am so sorry and so embarrassed,' she slurs. 'Let me help you out of those wet clothes,' she giggles.

She follows me through the union lounge and continues following me, even though I am clearly going into the gents to rinse off the carrots and peas that are stuck to my tee-shirt amongst the wet, rancid liquid. Despite a number of guys peeing into the communal urinal, she insists on accompanying me to the sink as I take off my tee-shirt.

'Wow, you are gorgeous. Do you work out?' she gasps.

Some of the guys washing their hands at the sink, turn around and smirk.

'This fresher seems to have pulled, eh lads!' exclaimed one.

Seems like she has done me a favour after all.

They come over, one of the guys pats me on the back and says, 'Welcome to freshers week, I'm Stu,' and pointing to the three other guys introduces them as Aaron, Steve, and Jim.

We walk back out towards the bar, leaving a very embarrassed looking girl in the gents' toilets.

The guys are second-year law students, could come in handy I think to myself. I make a special effort to contain any facial tics that have a tendency to develop when I am in new situations. Trying my utmost to act cool, I introduce myself to the guys, informing them of the unfortunate collision with fresher vomit.

The guys laugh with me and Aaron asks what my poison is.

Making a quick calculation, I tell them that I will get the first round in, hoping and praying the tenner in my pocket will cover it. Father taught me the sincerity of getting in the first round and developing trust, also, most people remember who got the first round in but rarely remembers who got the last.

Thankfully, the guys all order cider and the prices are unbelievably good. No wonder the majority of the students look hammered. I wouldn't be at all surprised if it isn't the first time some of the new students have been let off the leash. I dread to think how they will feel tomorrow, I hope their mate's rally round and help each other out. Mother had stayed by my bedside all night on the two occasions I was close to alcohol poisoning, something I will never forget.

Turns out, the guys no longer live on campus, they share a rented house with three other students, somewhere in Lenton. The halls of residence tend to be used by first year and mature students. This time next year I will need to rethink my accommodation. Time enough for that concern, best not obsess about it just yet.

The atmosphere begins to liven up further when the open mic session begins, making it impossible to have a conversation. My throat is already rasping from straining my vocal chords to shout above the noise and the constant inhalation of tobacco smoke.

I notice a familiar smell in the air, a smell that triggers a memory from not so many years ago. I visualise my friend Kenny, the same old image plays through my mind, Kenny injecting that fatal shot of heroin. My heart begins to race and sadness creeps over me like a spider weaving a web of depression, I begin to feel claustrophobic, almost suffocating as the web reaches my face rendering me breathless. With no time for explanation, I rush towards the door, hoping to catch my breath in the outside air. I feel a strange tingling in my arms and legs, but miraculously they are still working until I fall to my knees in the wet grass outside of the Students' Union bar. No one appears to be fazed by my behaviour. In fact, I am surrounded by other students in compromising positions, looking just as ill as I am.

It occurs to me that perhaps my unique behaviour, as Mother calls it, will not be such an issue here. I guess I will fit in with the crowd after all. I consider the trigger for my panic attack and come to the conclusion that the smell of the cannabis must have created an anxiety-producing situation. I will need to come to terms with this as I can only assume this may well be a regular occurrence, especially in the Students' Union bar and other communal areas. This is something I need to work on.

For a while, I sit on the wet grass watching the comings and goings of the other students as my heart rate begins to settle at a steadier pace and my breathing is less shallow. I observe the way the girls rally round, nurturing and caring for their sick friends and the guys how they laugh and make fun of their mates but at the same time discretely care for them. Jim and Steve find me on the grass, Jim gently punches me on the shoulder.

'Come on mate, I reckon you need something to eat.'

I follow them to one of the halls and into a student kitchen. Aaron is already there, smiling with a huge sausage sandwich in his hand, tomato ketchup squelching out of the sides. He calls us over.

'Plenty of sausages in the pan, go grab yourselves one. The bread is over there,' he says and points to a crumb covered countertop.

We all grab a sausage sandwich and check out the two girls who have entered the room. It just so happens that one of the girls is vomit girl who christened my tee-shirt earlier. She walks brazenly over to me, grabs my backside and snogs the tomato ketchup off my face. The other guys give a mighty 'whoa' as I catch my breath.

'I see we have a girl magnet amongst us,' laughed Steve.

'Hi, I'm Joy,' she said.

'You certainly are,' I answered. 'And I am Alfie, first-year Pharm student or I will be when classes start next week.'

Her friend hovered in the background. She looked embarrassed and shy; almost awkward. A feeling I recognised when I was on the periphery of the crowd when I felt an outsider. I smiled at her.

'And you are?'

'Also, a first-year Pharm student,' she answered. 'I'm Kate.'

As more students entered the room, the guys began networking their way around getting to know everyone. Personally, I can't cope with too much interaction at once and I would like to get to know a little more about Kate. I point to a scruffy dog eaten sofa and motion her to join me. We talk about the plans for tomorrow when we meet our tutors and are given a synopsis of the course. Kate appears to have done her homework, she informs me of the time and location we are to meet and surprisingly arranges to meet me outside of the lecture theatre the following day.

True to her word, Kate is waiting for me outside the designated lecture theatre. Vomit girl is nowhere to be seen. I consider asking Kate about the well-being of her friend, Joy, but decide against this for fear that this might be misinterpreted. Kate gave me a warm smile, nudged her shoulder against mine and raised her eyebrows.

'Let's do it. Now all will be revealed and we will know our fate, for the first year at least,' she joked.

The lecture theatre was already half full as we made our way to the front of the room.

'Hope you don't mind sitting so close to the front, Alfie, I have to admit that I can be a bit of a nerd when it comes to education. I'm very keen to follow in my Mother's footsteps and have every intention of working in research.'

I was intrigued. This girl was getting more interesting by the minute and she appeared to be as determined as me to achieve her dream. There is a gentle buzz of voices surrounding us. I check out the competition. We seem to be an interesting group of students. So far, the ratio of females to males appears to be evenly matched. My train of thought is broken as one of the members of the faculty makes her way to the podium and taps a metal pointy stick onto the surface. To my amazement, she flips the stick making it unfold. I realise it is a car aerial. How ingenious!

Instantly the hush of voices settles down. Just as the room is audibly quiet, the lecture theatre door is abruptly opened and Joy enters the room shouting our names, waving her hands frantically in the air.

Kate hangs her head in shame so it is left to me to wave back at Joy if nothing more than to quieten her down.

She runs down to the front to join us and ignoring the tip-tapping of the aerial against the podium, whispers to me, 'Why the hell have you come to the front?'

I ignore her remark and smile weakly at the member of the faculty, who has yet to introduce herself. So here I am, sandwiched between Kate and Joy. How did this happen? I need to get to know some of the guys in my group if I am to survive this course. I sit for two hours while we are presented with the fundamentals of the curriculum and an introduction to the staff. Finally, after being told of the rules and regulations of the university and the campus, we are dismissed. I noticed that the majority of the students had been making notes, including Kate. Joy, on the other hand, just sat there and appeared to be on another planet. It had never occurred to me, to bring a notebook. That doesn't mean to say that I wasn't interested enough, quite the contrary. I was paying attention alright. All of the bullet points were stored away in my head, ready to be retrieved as needed.

It appears that for the remainder of the day we were free to peruse our own interests. I made my excuses to Kate and Joy, with the intention of going to the student bookshop to purchase some of the books we had been recommended to buy, for our first year of study. It feels like a different world walking around the campus, almost surreal and so far removed from school, where I still felt like a child. Here I feel free and dare I think it, I feel unique. Not in the same way as feeling different because of my tics and alternate behaviour. This is a more powerful feeling. I think that maybe expressing oneself in an alternative way is probably more acceptable here.

As I look around me, I notice students displaying their own individuality. Some of the guys have long hair, some are wearing bandannas around their heads. Most are casually dressed and some are verging on downright scruffy. There is such a cross-section of students here. I have a positive feeling; I think I am going to be alright.

CHAPTER THIRTY

Grace's Diary

29 NOVEMBER 1996

The house feels empty without Alfie. He has only been away a couple of months, but it feels like an eternity. When I wake up in the morning, the house is quiet. No longer do I hear the squeaking from the mattress as Alfie tosses and turns restlessly in his sleep. He has never been a good sleeper; I am worried how he is coping in his new environment.

His morning rituals became my own habits. They are ingrained into my own behaviour. I still have my shower and get dressed before going downstairs to open the curtains. When Alfie was small, he insisted that the curtains remained closed until we were both up and dressed. If I was the first downstairs, the curtains remained closed until we were both ready to face the day. Alfie always needed to be the one who opened the curtains, it became an obsession of his, one that I played along with. I learned this when he was around four-years-old, he had already begun to develop obsessive tendencies and repetitive behaviour patterns. I had got into the habit of playing along with these, to avoid the tantrums and screaming when a routine was broken. It took me a while to realise that Alfie wasn't being naughty, he was truly distressed. Sometimes it was difficult for me to cope with his behaviour, but with time, most of his obsessions became manageable and were well hidden from others.

When he first left home, I sat quietly, alone, at the breakfast table drinking my tea, but not enjoying it. My routine is all out of key and my life feels out of focus. I have started listening to the radio every day, tuning in to the local radio station to catch up on all of the local gossip and events. The hosts on the radio are like pseudo-friends. Their happy, friendly banter breaks the overwhelming silence of my home. A silence that suffocates me.

Hazel always seems to know what is happening locally before it is announced on the radio. I'm beginning to wonder if she tunes into those citizen band radio frequencies or if she is having an affair with a local journalist. Either way, she appears to know more gossip than anyone I know. She sometimes pops round for a coffee and a chat. Her life is so different from mine in terms of her having more time on her hands to socialise and have fun. Hazel still works part-time at the Co-op and frequently tries to persuade me to go out with her for a drink and a game of bingo. Truthfully, that is not for me, but in the name of friendship, I have been to the cinema a few times with her and called for a drink afterwards. She understands that I prefer not to call in at the Welfare Club for a drink in case we see Paul with his wife. It's not that I am still angry or jealous, it's more a preservation thing.

Lately, my job has become very demanding, leaving me little time to socialize. Although, I do make a point of inviting Mum and Dad round for Sunday lunch. Sometimes Pam joins us, although very rarely now because she is in a new relationship. Her partner, Eric, takes her out for Sunday lunch most weeks. He is very kind and generous with her. Sometimes I am ashamed to say that I feel envious. I have willingly sacrificed everything for Alfie and would not have it any other way, but sometimes I feel as if my life is passing me by.

These days I feel too tired to do anything other than sit on the sofa after work with a glass of wine and watch mindless television programmes. When I think about the energy I used to have and the drive to study and pass my diploma. I sometimes think where has that woman gone? How anyone has the energy to go out after work baffles me.

Mum and Dad keep encouraging me to date, I wonder if they will ever give up. They keep pointing out men to me, including their new bank manager, who apparently is also divorced. I never expected my life to turn out like this. However, I am very proud of my accomplishments. I am the only one in the family with a diploma and our Pam is very envious of my career in dietetics! Since Alfie is no longer at home, I have become lazy and I no longer cook proper dinners. I don't have much appetite or energy, so I just make myself quick, light meals.

3 JANUARY 1997

I found the energy to go out on New Year's Eve with Pam and Eric but I had to hide how exhausted I was from them. They looked so happy together. They were singing and dancing together; having the time of their life. At one point, Pam actually climbed onto a table and started to twist away to an old Chubby Checker song. It was good to see her having such fun. They tried so hard to include me. So, I tried my utmost but I know something is wrong and I don't want anyone to fuss over me. I keep getting painful, horrible kidney infections that require antibiotics and which take longer to recover from each time.

Most evenings when I get home from work, I am so tired and drained I just want to collapse on the sofa. I have even started eating ready-made meals. Alfie tends to ring me quite late in the evening and sometimes I find I have already nodded off to sleep in the chair. I swear one of these nights I will end up spending the whole night there.

He seems to be settling in at university quite well and talks enthusiastically about the course content. It appears that he has made a few friends, I think one is called Stu. He also mentioned a girl called Kate, she sounds a nice and she is on the same course as him. When I enquired if romance was on the horizon, he went quiet and said that although there was room in his heart, Magenta was still there and he was not quite ready to replace her yet. My sweet boy. I worry that he will never get over his first love.

CHAPTER THIRTY-ONE

Alfie

Mother seems to be hoping against all odds that I will form a relationship with Kate. To be honest, I'm not sure if that is what Kate wants. I get the impression that she prefers male company, but not from a romantic perspective. She doesn't appear to get on well with other girls. She once told me that most of them were silly bimbos, more interested in boys, make-up, and fashion than actually getting down to some serious study. Her reason for hanging with me was as a smokescreen to keep the girls away so that she was not distracted. In addition, she hoped the other guys would consider her as being involved with me.

At first, I felt used. Then I began to believe that it could work this to my advantage. Altruism can be beneficial for both parties. If you like, it is a win/win situation, providing we both continue, to get what we want from each other.

Magenta was still very much in my heart and mind. I could not shake off her memory, but I could succeed with my degree for both of us and for my parents who had sacrificed so much to get me this far.

Joy, on the other hand, was practically offering herself on a plate to me. The first few months at university I witnessed the coupling up of students that would make Sodom and Gomorrah appear tame. I began to wonder how anyone managed to get any revision time in. Some days Joy didn't attend the lectures. On the days she did, she always sat at the back of the lecture theatre, while Kate and I continued to sit at the front. Kate scribbling away in her notebook and me soaking up every spoken word.

From time to time I met up with Steve and the gang, mostly in the Students' Union bar. They were a great group of guys and although they teased me about my tics when they were more noticeable at times of stress. I took it all as good fun and banter. One weekend they invited me to join them at Rock City, a live music venue in the city centre.

'You will fit right in mate, with your weird dark clothes,' joked Aaron.

So, I went along with the guys one night and who should be there to pounce on me at the end of the night but Joy. She was absolutely smashed out of her head and coming onto me as though I was some sort of sex god. The guys thought it was hilarious and encouraged me to take her up on her kind offer. Although I had no intention of taking advantage of a very drunk woman. I did leave with Joy, but only to make sure that she got safely back to her halls. This was not easy as Joy was struggling to walk. At one point she stopped, leaned against the nearest lamp post and true to her nickname of vomit girl, threw up. I swear I have never seen vomit shoot so far, such was the force of her young body rejecting whatever substance she had ingested.

It took me two hours to get Joy back to the campus and into her halls. After fumbling in her bag for ages, she found the key to her room and with trembling hands passed it to me. I helped her onto the bed and laid her on her left side. She looked so young and vulnerable. I carefully removed her ridiculously high-heel shoes and put them neatly on the floor. Thinking back to my own experience of an alcohol-induced stupor, when Mother stayed with me all night, I decided that the safest thing to do was to keep watch on her all night. So, I grabbed some cushions from the bed and lay on the floor. I remained there all night, waking up only when Joy stepped on me as she climbed out of bed. I don't know who was more surprised, me or her as I felt her sudden weight against my abdomen.

Joy just managed to get to the sink in time for the first round of vomit to splatter against the white porcelain. I held her hair away from her face and supported her thin trembling body. Having helped Joy back to bed, I propped her up with pillows, then left the room discretely or so I thought. Who should be making their way towards the kitchen for an early morning cuppa? Yes, it was Kate. If looks could kill I would surely be a dead man now. There was no point explaining; why should I? What I did do was request that she pop in to check that Joy was alright, this even coming from my lips seemed a strange request, because, by all accounts, I looked as guilty as hell.

I returned to my own room and climbed wearily into bed. No one in our block would be awake for hours, after all, it was Sunday, a day of rest or a day of revision. I woke mid-morning, my mouth as dry as sandpaper. I flicked the switch on the travel kettle that Mother had kindly bought me and found a carton of long life milk and some instant coffee that I kept on the top of the chest of drawers. I'm not too keen on long life milk, but it will have to do. The remainder of the day I dedicated to my studies, preparing for the practical work which was planned for the following day. I read a huge amount of subject matter, willing it to soak into my memory. I very rarely make notes and have always struggled with writing. I do enjoy the visuals, though, for some reason I find it relatively easy to remember and memorise whole chunks of films, in particular, the ones with a distinct soundtrack. My brain tunes into rhyme and rhythm. Respective sequencing easily makes its way into my long-term memory and I regularly make rhymes up in my head of whole chunks of information that I need to retain.

Around six o'clock, I make my way to the Students' Union bar. I fancy a burger and chips. Mother would be horrified if she knew this was my Sunday dinner. I guess she will be having a roast with all the trimmings and maybe my grandparents will be around to keep her company. I do hope so. When I ring home later, it is a while before the phone is answered and when she does, she sounds sleepy, as though I have just woken her and yet it is only nine o'clock.

As soon as she realises it is me on the line, her tone of voice changes and rises an octave. I can tell she is pretending to be fine as she breezily enquires about my day. I never give her too much information and only ever discuss the positive parts of my life at university. Eventually, I get the opportunity to ask about herself, she gives away very little information except that she is currently on her second round of antibiotics for a kidney infection that is not responding to treatment. I enquire if she is off sick from work, Mother very rarely takes sick leave and when she admits to me that she has been off work since the middle of the week. I know that she is definitely not well.

I ask if she wants me to come home to help her, but she flatly refuses and insists that I stay exactly where I am and not to miss any lectures.

I wish her goodnight and not for the first time today, I worry about Joy and how she is feeling and now I have the added worry of Mother.

Although it is getting late, I make my way to the female halls with the intention of checking on Joy. I have no romantic notions about her, even if she has for me, but I consider her a mate and that's what mates do. I wonder that it might seem a little forward if I make my way directly to her room, so I head to the common room, just in case she is chilling in there. Joy is not in the common room, but some of the other students are. I enquire if anyone has seen her today. They all look a bit shifty and start to shuffle around.

One of the girls, whose name I don't know, came across to me and said that I should keep well clear of Joy as she wasn't wired up right and was definitely trouble.

Now, where have I heard that before? How many times in the past, has the same been said about me? No one wanted to be my friend and I always felt on the periphery. If I hadn't been blessed with the kind of looks that the girls go for, even some of the guys, then I would still be treated like a social outcast. Perhaps I had got it all wrong with Joy. Maybe her attention seeking behaviour hid something much deeper and instead of being angry with her I should pity her and try to understand what is driving her to self-destruct.

I make my way towards Joy's room. I'm not sure how to handle this and I begin to feel an old familiar feeling surge through my body. My right hand begins to flap about, so I try and steady it with my left hand. This works for all of two seconds, at which point, my jaw tightens up and instinctively I grind my back teeth. It is not until I enter the already half-open door of her room that reality dawns on me. Joy is sat crossed legs on her bed, smoking a rolled-up joint. I feel the nausea rise-up into my throat as the acid reflux hits my mouth. She doesn't even glance in my direction. For a moment, I consider turning around and getting away as fast as my feet would carry me, then I remember the reason why I am here and why I must overcome the panic and the distant memories of Kenny.

I think Joy was expecting me to do just that. To walk away and abandon her. It is likely that she has experienced this kind of behaviour many times. I am not sorry to disappoint her.

'You are still here then?' she whispers. 'I should escape pretty sharpish if I were you, best not be associated with me. I'm a loser and apparently always will be.'

I am saddened to hear her defeatist words and all the more determined to help her through whatever is causing her pain. She glances down at my flapping hands and registers the tightness of my jaw. She holds out the joint, her hand trembling as the ash drops to the floor.

'I think you need this more than me Alfie,' she whispers.

I shake my head, but take it out of her hand. I stub out the joint, then climb onto the bed at the side of her. As I do, she begins to cry, leaning against my shoulder, she sobs and sobs until finally she looks up at me and asks me to tell her my story. Without hesitation, I tell her about my childhood and how I stood by and watched my Father with another woman, whom he eventually left my Mother for.

I tell her of my difficulty making friendships and how I was different from the other children. Then I tell her about Kenny and how he died. What I don't mention is Mags. And the terrible things that happened to her. She listens without interruption. When I have finished she wants to know more, about Mother.

'Do you love your mother Alfie?' she bluntly asks.

'Of course, with all of my heart. I owe her so much,' is my honest reply.

I consider the question and ask if she loves her own mother.

Joy looks me straight in the eyes and replies that she hates her mother and never wants to see her again.

To say I am surprised is an understatement. I cannot begin to imagine what a mother could have done to deserve such a profound feeling of hate and resentment. Joy does not elaborate further, instead, she seems to be shrinking inside of herself, closing off as though the conversation has ended. I can see that our discussion is somehow unsettling her, which was not my intention. Remembering something I had read in psychology about distraction therapy, I grabbed her hand and ask her to come with me for a walk around the grounds to blow away the cobwebs, as my Mother would say. Surprisingly, she agreed, so we left the halls together as many prying eyes peered out from the common room window. No doubt Kate's included.

CHAPTER THIRTY-TWO

Grace's Diary

16 APRIL 1997

I am happy that Alfie is so settled at university. I have heard many stories of how children are home every weekend with their washing and ironing, but Alfie is either the filthiest student at university or the most broke and he can't afford the fare home. He has surprised me and yes, he has made me proud. Alfie knows he can come home anytime he wants, day or night without question and if he really is broke, he only has to ask for money. His phone calls are random. I suppose that can be a good thing. Saves me from disappointment if I was to expect a call and he let me down.

His pharmacology degree appears to be going well. He tells me that he is due to take some mock exams soon. When I enquired if he was weak in any of the subject areas, Alfie remarked that weakness was for losers and no way was he ever going to be a loser. Interesting perspective, I thought. I guess he is managing to get on with his studies without any worry from home to distract him. This is exactly how I want things to remain. I never discuss any negative issues from this end, even though my own health has been thrown into question recently.

I have been referred to the nephrology clinic at the hospital. Something about a declining glomerular filtration rate. I think it refers to the rate that my kidneys are functioning. Alfie needn't know and providing he gives me warning of a visit, I can manage to put on a good act of being well when he is here. I am getting better at keeping my declining health a secret, even my parents don't seem to notice. Sometimes I feel invisible; I don't think anybody sees how exhausted I am.

I have spent years being strong for Alfie. Working hard and developing a successful career. I don't want anyone to see me as weak, I don't want them to say, 'Oh look at how pathetic Grace is.' So, I have decided to keep my illness a secret. I will manage it myself. I am fine on my own; I can cope. As Alfie has started saying, 'weakness is for losers.'

9 MAY 1997

I forced myself to go out with my work colleagues for a leaving do. It was at Antico Restaurant where Alfie and Magenta used to work. Mr Rossi, the manager asked after Alfie and was very friendly with me. In fact, my colleague Susan hinted that he was flirting with me. I had attempted to make an effort and I even treated myself to a new dress for the occasion, seeing as most of my clothes were too big for me.

I really enjoyed the meal and spending time socialising with my colleagues. I wish that I had done it sooner. I couldn't drink wine due to the antibiotics that I was taking. Susan wanted to know why I wouldn't share a bottle of red wine with her, so I lied and said that I wouldn't even have a small glass and drive my car. I think that I have been managing to hide my illness from everyone quite well. I can battle it myself without all the false sympathies that people give.

I have started reading some medical journals to try and understand my illness better and it has helped expand my knowledge of medicine further. Alfie is very impressed that I can comprehend his university work. He calls some evenings and talks to me about what he has learnt in his lectures. Alfie is very enthusiastic about pharmacology and obsessively talks about how the different compounds in medicine work together. He tells me about agonists and inhibitors, analgesics and beta blockers. I can tell from the excitement and wonder in his voice that he finds the world of pharmacology fascinating. Although he rarely discusses any of his friendships, he did recently tell me that his friend Kate has done a U-turn and he will never understand women. I didn't pry, it is for Alfie to decide when he wants to share his emotional feelings. I am on standby if the occasion should arise.

CHAPTER THIRTY-THREE

Alfie

I have started hanging out with Aaron, Steve, and the other guys at the weekends. I know I really should go home and visit Mother more often, but I am having such a good time, I'm sure she understands.

Father and Rose have written to me regularly as promised. They tell me that nothing changes much in the village. The men at his local Miner's Welfare Club ask about me apparently and Father proudly tells them that one day I will be working in medicine. He has started writing to me as Dr Alf, even though I have explained on a number of occasions that I need a PhD to be entitled to use Dr before my name.

He never refers to my problems and the repetitive behaviours I still suffer from. The truth is, that for most of the time I can keep my strangeness, as my grandparents call it, well hidden. It is only at times of stress that I find this difficult. In my own room, my space, my books are lined up neatly, colour coordinated, there is only me to open the curtains and I can place all my toiletries in alphabetical order without anyone really noticing.

I still have strange, frightening dreams and thoughts, which I am learning to control. When these thoughts invade my space, I imagine the voices are just a record playing in the background of my mind. I overcome this by distraction therapy, using alternative thoughts which are louder and more positive than the negative, frightening voices in my head. Sometimes I think that perhaps my brain is not wired up like everyone else's. It is as though the two halves of my brain, although connected, seem to have a short circuit of some kind.

Next year, we are studying the brain, biology and function. Maybe this will help me to understand more about what makes me so different. I am very interested in the way different neurotransmitter chemicals work in the brain and the influence of how cytotoxic chemicals modify and change behaviour.

In our third year, we will be investigating the modes of actions of drugs at molecular levels and how the drugs are absorbed, metabolised and excreted. It is so interesting and relevant. I feel fortunate to be given this opportunity. The educational side of my life comes to me so naturally. However, I still have to work on my social skills. I try very hard to be social and be seen as one of the guys, truly, it does not come naturally to me and I have to make a real effort. So, when Aaron asked me to join the campus football team for a bit of fun, having played in a team before, I jumped at the chance. When they saw me in the goal they couldn't believe their eyes, now I am training three times a week.

Joy is on the sidelines every match, cheering the team on. It has been a good team building experience, helped by the fact that there are some third-year pharm students on the team. Very useful for advice on what to expect for the remainder of the year in terms of expectations from the faculty. Next week, I have invited Steve and Aaron to come home with me for the weekend and meet Mother. I have told them what an amazing cook she is; I know that she won't let me down.

Joy is just a mate, almost one of the lads now. We have a lot in common. She also had a tough time at school and didn't make friends easily. However, unlike me, Joy also had an unhappy home life. She was sent to one psychiatrist after the other. She was put on a number of different medications, all with unwanted side effects and is currently on anti-depressants.

Joy's birth was not expected. Her mother was already in her mid-forties and had never wanted children. Apparently, by the time she realised that she was pregnant with Joy, it was too late to do anything about it. Her father was secretly delighted to have a daughter and practically raised her himself. She describes her mother as being bitter and angry, using any excuse to berate Joy. It was her father who encouraged her with her studies and being gifted with a photographic memory, she had no problems with exams, leaving school with four A stars in the science subjects.

Unknown to Joy and much to her mother's annoyance, her father had set up a trust fund for her university years with enough to provide a small income for the next fifteen years, by which time he hoped she would be well established in pharmacology. Sadly, her father died suddenly just after her place at the University of Nottingham had been confirmed. Joy was still trying to come to terms with his loss and at the same time defend her father's decision in terms of the financial provision he had made. Apparently, her mother was contesting the will and putting emotional pressure on Joy. This explained her desperate behaviour in the first few weeks at university. She was not used to drinking alcohol, which interacted with her prescribed medication. No surprises then that she appeared so uncontrolled.

I no longer call her vomit girl. She laughed when I told her of this nickname and has now forgiven me. I find it hard to believe that her own mother could be so unkind. My mother has made sacrifice after sacrifice for me, even her own happiness she put at risk. I suspect that she still loves Father. It makes me terribly sad to see her alone and I know she puts on a brave face when I visit her, but I see beyond the mask that she paints on her face, I see the pain in her eyes. She taught me that the eyes are the windows to the soul, I guess she means that a person's emotions can be reflected in their eyes.

I am still hoping to see Mags and when that day comes and it will, no matter how long it takes, no matter how old and tired my eyes become, they will light up and dance with the brightest and happiest emotions. Until then, I am concentrating on my future, awaiting whatever fate has in store.

CHAPTER THIRTY-FOUR

Grace's Diary

2 JULY 1997

Alfie is coming home this weekend and bringing two friends to stay. I can't wait as it feels like months since I have seen him. However, I have some reservations with respect to the extra work this will entail for me.

I have managed to hide my declining health from him so far and I don't want him to see how unwell I feel. I need to keep working so that I can afford for him to stay in university. I don't want anyone to encourage me to take sick leave or even change my hours to work part-time. Otherwise, I cannot afford to pay for Alfie's tuition fees and towards his living expenses. I know Paul sends him a bit of money each month and he has the emergency money from my parents, but it will not be enough. I never did ask Alfie how much of his own money he managed to save from the work he had been doing. Still, that's his business. Maybe I am worrying unnecessarily so.

I need to keep it a secret until he completes university. I don't want Alfie to see how unwell I feel, so the preparations will need to start early. I have already prepared the beds with fresh linen and placed bath towels and toiletries out for them. I will prepare the food in stages and get plenty of nibbles and snacks in for them. I hope Alfie doesn't bring too much washing home as the weather has been very unpredictable and drying it all may prove impossible. I think the time has come to invest in a tumble dryer, that way I won't have to hang the washing outside on the line as even that exhausts me these days.

I'm feeling anxious. I am scared of having to give up work due to this stupid illness. I have to conserve my energy for work as it is my only source of income. Without it, Alfie will really struggle. I don't want him taking on a student loan. I have heard stories of young students leaving university with a mountain of debt. Paul does his best, but he has other responsibilities. My heart aches when I remember our early years of marriage and the struggle we had to conceive Alfie. At times, I spiral into a low mood, verging on depression, when I reminisce. In addition, my parents are becoming frail, as is expected at their age. I have successfully kept my kidney disease a secret from everyone. However, I think some people at work are starting to become suspicious. Pam has also started to take a sudden interest in my health. Every time she visits me, I can feel her scrutinising me. She keeps commenting on how baggy my clothes are. I know it's because she cares about me, but even so, it's a constant reminder of my condition.

I have been referred to a specialist called a nephrologist, he says it is only a matter of time before my kidneys fail altogether. He explained the different management plans. I am currently on medication and a restricted protein diet. He has warned me that eventually, I will need dialysis. I'm worried about how this will affect my working life and whether or not I'll even be able to work whilst on this form of dialysis. He spoke of peritoneal dialysis which can be done at home. The next stage is kidney dialysis at the hospital until a donor becomes available. He asked me to consider this and plan accordingly. It was a huge shock to be hearing that my life depends on finding a suitable kidney donor. I just need to get Alfie through university, then maybe I can reduce my hours at work. I might suggest to Paul that he spends some time with Alfie and his friends on Sunday, that will give me the opportunity to prepare a dinner. I feel mean, but I won't be inviting my parents as well, not this week at least. I don't think I could cope with six for dinner. I hope they understand. Perhaps Alfie might call to visit them next time he is over for the weekend?

CHAPTER THIRTY-FIVE

Paul

Grace is ill. I know she is, although there is no way she will admit it to me or anyone else. I am not sure if it is women's problems or something worse. She looks so tired when I see her in the Co-op doing the shopping. The last time I saw her, she looked as though she didn't have the strength to push the shopping trolley and there were only a few items in it. In fact, I swear that she has lost even more weight since I last saw her a month ago. Her clothes are hanging off her and she has a funny colour to her face.

I know how much I hurt Grace in the past and nothing will ever change that. It was so long ago, times were different, we were caught up in the strike action and I was young and foolish. I know that now, but I cannot change history. I was dragged along without any thought for my actions or their consequences. Sometimes, the regret I feel seems to wedge itself like a bolus of chewed food stuck in my gullet. If only I could change history I would have been a better man, a husband that Grace truly deserved and a father who was strong enough to love and support his son unconditionally. Perhaps one day I can be absolved for betraying my family when they needed me.

Grace would never hurt anyone, she is a good woman. I should have stood by and supported her with Alfie. The only good thing that has come out of this is Rose. She is a fine girl. I see some of Alfie in her and I think that she will do well. Her two older step-brothers are a nightmare. They are older than Alfie by a few years and the only way I can describe them is as fat and lazy. Neither of them has a fraction of the intelligence that Alfie and Rose possess and have no intention of finding a job. They spend most of their time in front of the television watching sport, which makes me smile as they don't have a sporting bone in their bodies. Unlike Alfie, I used to get such a good feeling watching him play football. He came alive on that football pitch. It didn't matter that he was different to the rest of the team and his social skills were limited, I know he found interaction with his own peer group difficult. He always appeared to interact better with the older children. I guess that his own age group bored him. I remember him looking blank at them when they behaved in a childish way. It was as though he had a missing link. His mind is always so matter of fact, so literal. Alfie seems to struggle to understand questions that are phrased in a certain way.

I remember Grace telling him that we were having his grand-parents for dinner. He looked horrified and said that he would rather have roast chicken. He once asked me why people don't say what they mean? Why don't they get straight to the point instead of talking in riddles? Sadly, I wasn't able to explain this to my son, it is just the way some people speak around here. I guess he will figure this out for himself one day.

Sometimes I question my role as his father. I know that I let him down badly and for that I am ashamed. I tried to help him to develop an interest in topics that normal kids talked about, but he found mundane chit chat so boring. Not that any of that matters now, in fact, it has become an advantage in the adult world. I presume the professors at the university are very literal and matter of fact, so finally, our Alfie is in good company.

Rose and I write to him every month, although he writes back, his letters are quite short and always matter of fact. No embellishments or sentiments, but that is who he is and I love him for it. I think he will make a fine career in pharmacology and medicine if his terrible writing is anything to go by.

CHAPTER THIRTY-SIX

Alfie

I t felt so good to be home in my own bedroom. Mother hasn't changed a thing, other than my bed sheets that is. I found it comforting looking around at the familiar surroundings. Of course, a lot of the things in my room, I have long grown out of, but I can't bear to move them. All of my football trophies are on the shelf, lined up in size order. Steve and Aaron were astonished to see my silver cups and the photographs of me in the local newspaper. They joked about how tidy it was, with everything in straight lines, colour coded or in alphabetical order. I laughed with them as I have learned to do. I am well aware of my idiosyncrasies, there is no point in denying these traits. It is part of who I am and providing I don't get stressed or overtired, my tics are barely noticeable.

The guys are bunked up in the spare bedroom next to mine and soon made themselves at home. As expected, there was a delicious cooking smell drifting from the kitchen as we entered through the front door.

'Mm! Bisto!' said Aaron.

I could almost see his mouth watering.

Mother called us through to the dining room and after a quick introduction, we dropped our rucksacks to the floor and between us, we devoured a dish full of the most delicious goulash with creamy mashed potatoes. I noticed that Mother ate very little, perhaps she had something earlier?

We soon made ourselves comfortable in front of the television to watch the Saturday afternoon sport and check out the football results. I remember when I was very young, Father used to do the football pools and every Saturday we all sat together hoping and praying for seven draws. We daydreamed about what we would do with the winnings. Mothers' dream was to live in the countryside with a nice cottage and a small holding where she would grow her own vegetables and have chickens. There were to be roses around the door, just like in fairy tales. Father had a different dream. He wanted to move to Australia and have a ranch with sheep and horses. He said it was the land of opportunity.

My dream was always the same dream. To be like other boys and to stop the thoughts turning constantly around in my mind, giving me no peace and disturbing my sleep. I didn't know then, but I know now, that no amount of money can rewire my brain.

The guys wanted me to show them the town and some of the local pubs. Our town is still a fun place to be, with lots of pubs and nightclubs and on a Saturday night, it is usually rammed. To-night, was no exception. The town was full of youngsters and I swear some of them were no older than thirteen, all pretending to be grown up, as I did at that age. We did the circuit, a proper pub crawl around the town. I saw a few familiar faces in the crowd, but as always, the one familiar face I was looking for was nowhere to be seen. I think the guys enjoyed the night. When we got home, Mother was already in bed. She left us a video to watch and lots of snacks and beers on the coffee table. I guess she knows what us lads are like and gave us our privacy.

Sunday morning Mother was up before us. I knew this because I could smell the bacon cooking. She called up the stairs and asked how we all wanted our eggs cooking. Bleary-eyed, we slowly made our way to the table, each of us hungover from the night before. That was my excuse for the way we looked, but I was surprised to see that Mother looked worse than either of us. Her eyes looked puffy and swollen and her skin was very pale and unhealthy looking. Instead of the usual spring to her gait, she was slow and clumsy. I hadn't really taken much notice the previous day, but now she had my full attention. I didn't like what I saw, even with my limited medical knowledge I recognised that Mother was not well.

After breakfast, the guys made themselves comfortable in front of the television. I stayed in the kitchen to help Mother clear away the breakfast pots, it provided me with an opportunity to ask after her health. As expected, she tried to brush away any concerns and said that all she needed was a good holiday, perhaps some sea air.

I suggested that maybe she could go to the East Coast with Aunty Pam, but Mother seemed to think that was out of the question. Then I thought that it might be nice for her to go with Grandmother and Grandfather, to which she just smiled and said,

'I don't think so, Alfie dear, that would be too exhausting for me.'

I think I will have a word with Father later. We are to watch a local football team play in the Sunday League and have a pint in the Welfare Club with his mates afterwards. I have prepared Steve and Aaron to expect some leg pulling from the old guys, especially when they know that they are studying law. I am expecting a fanfare when I walk into the Welfare Club, the way Father has bragged about his only son going to university.

I had to smile when we walked into the crowded pub, with the tables all lined up in rows and swilling in beer. As usual, one of the ex-miners was touting for business, selling raffle tickets in aid of the old folks and the children's Christmas party. At one table, a group of old men was playing dominoes. Father got us all a pint of Mansfield ale and enquired if we fancied a game of darts. To be fair, it was good fun and Aaron became quite competitive with Father, who only just managed to win by the skin of his teeth.

As we made our way home, I spoke with Father about my concerns for Mother. He tried to reassure me, but I looked at his sorrowful eyes. His words were saying one thing, but his face was saying another. I decided not to pursue the subject any further. When we arrived home from the pub, noisy and full of spirit, Mother was still busy in the kitchen. She called out to make ourselves comfortable in the lounge and she would call when the dinner was to be served. The guys did as she asked. After twenty hungry minutes, I popped my head surreptitiously around the kitchen door. Mother was sat at the table, holding her head in her hands. She sounded breathless, her shoulders were rising and falling at an unusual rate.

I felt panicked as I walked over to her. The rising panic sent a weird tingle up my spine. My left knee began to shake and I felt like something was crawling up my back. Taking a deep breath, I reached out to Mother, putting my hand on her rising and falling shoulders. She turned to face me, her mouth opened and closed like a fish out of water. I ran to open the kitchen windows and turned off the cooker. Loosening Mother's blouse buttons, I shouted out to the guys to ring for an ambulance. I heard Aaron on the phone as Steve made his way into the kitchen. Together we lifted Mother up and carried her to the sofa in the living room. I raised her legs high above her heart, propped her up on the sofa with lots of scatter cushions and gently held her hand, all the time talking to her and telling her that help was on its way.

I felt the panic rise-up inside me like a tsunami. The words tumbling out of my mouth sounded strange and unreal to me, as in the distance I heard the ambulance sirens approaching. When the paramedics arrived, they immediately put an oxygen mask on Mother and lifted her onto a stretcher. They enquired if she was on any medication. I realised that I had no idea, but I could guess where she would store them if there was any. I had not been inside Mother's room for years. It felt intrusive going into this private place of hers and even more so, going through her drawers. I was shocked to find a cocktail of medicines with Mother's name on them. I was familiar with some of the names. She was on Angiotensive converting enzymes, steroids, antibiotics, and ferrous sulphate iron tablets. I ran downstairs, clutching all of the medicines with her name on them.

'Do you want to come with us?' asked the paramedic as he climbed into the back of the ambulance.

I shook my head and said that I would be along shortly.

Aaron and Steve patted me on the back as we walked into the house. I suggested they check out the dinner and help themselves, while I contacted my grandparents. It was some time before I heard the click on the other end of the line and heard the old, familiar voice of Grandfather.

I explained the situation. For a short while, there was no reply and I thought that maybe the line had gone dead.

Then he said that I was not to worry, he would contact Aunty Pam to pick them up from their home and he would meet me at the hospital later.

I returned to the kitchen, my arms were twitching uncontrollably. Steve looked at me like I was from another planet, but Aaron came over to me.

'You're in shock, mate. Come over here and sit down. Take a few deep breaths and allow yourself time to recover. There is no hurry. We can help, can't we Steve?'

I looked over to Steve, who was stuffing his face with the food that Mother had prepared for us. He nodded in agreement and continued to eat. Aaron fetched me a drink of water, which I sipped slowly, trying to rationalise the situation. As my heart rate began to steady, my head felt clear enough to begin to take control of the situation.

I told Aaron to help himself to dinner. I was no longer hungry so I quickly cleared away the cooking pots and placed the leftovers in a covered dish. When the guys had finished eating, I rang a taxi to take them to the train station and asked them to somehow let my tutor know that I would most likely be away for at least a week or maybe longer. I suggested that they might let Joy know, then she could pass on the message.

When Steve and Aaron left, they said to thank Mother for her wonderful hospitality and wished her a speedy recovery.

Left alone in the house, my home, the overwhelming quietness seemed surreal. My mother, the heart and soul of my life was ill. In retrospect, I realised that it was likely that she had been ill for some time and had kept it from me. I understand her reasons. As always, she put everyone but herself first. Once again, I entered my Mother's bedroom. This time to collect some night clothes and toiletries. It felt intrusive, going through her underwear and night-wear. It felt so very wrong. I gathered a few toiletries and a towel from the bathroom tipped everything out of my rucksack and put Mother's belongings neatly inside.

Public transport is very infrequent in our village, especially on Sundays. So, I had no choice, but to phone for a taxi. This weekend was beginning to cost me a lot of money. Although the beer in the

Welfare Club was a fair price, the pub crawl last night and the entrance fee to the club had left me skint. I had no choice but to try and find Mother's purse and help myself to a loan, one that I hoped to somehow pay back later. It was not hard to find, but there was very little cash inside, hopefully enough for a one-way journey and maybe Aunty Pam would give me a lift home.

Unsure exactly where Mother was to be taken, I guessed that the best place to start was probably the accident and emergency department. The taxi fare was less than expected, which was a great relief.

Anxiously I make my way through the sliding doors. The smell of disinfectant fills the air, followed by the smell of sweat and fear. The waiting area is extremely busy and noisy. Children are crying and grown men are hobbling around. I notice a couple of guys still wearing their football boots, who have likely been playing in the Sunday League. Nurses and orderlies are racing from one cubicle to another and porters are expertly moving trolleys around with sick and injured patients tucked neatly under the cellular blankets. I go to the main reception desk to inquire if Mother has been seen.

After shuffling a few papers around, the receptionist informs me that she has been transferred to the female medical ward on the upper floor of the hospital.

While waiting for the lift, I hear a familiar shuffle of feet as my Grandfather, shuffles up the corridor. A short distance behind him is Aunty Pam, propping up Grandmother, as she hobbles slowly along. I feel a huge lump rise in my throat and a heavy pain in my chest.

When did they get so old and frail, how can this be?

I hold my hand out to steady Grandfather as he approaches the lift. It is only then that he recognises me, which startles him, making him catch his breath.

'Well, if it isn't our Alfie!' he shouts to Aunty Pam. 'Look, it's our young Alfie.'

Together we go up to the female medical ward, all of us with heavy hearts. Grandfather hangs on to my arm and Grandmother hangs on to Aunty Pam as we make our way down Abbott Ward towards the sister's office. A member of staff directs us to a side ward where we see Mother propped up in bed with an oxygen mask on her face. She turns to face us as we enter the room and lifts the mask, resting it on her forehead as the oxygen continues to hiss its way out of the mask. She gives us all a weak smile and holds out her hand to gesture us to come closer.

'Please don't worry. It is nothing serious, no more than a kidney infection. I will recover.'

Her parents, my grandparents, had been around too long to accept her words, but graciously did so, as did I. However, Aunty Pam was having none of it and said as much. I could see that this was distressing Mother further.

I leaned over and returned the oxygen mask to her face, held her hand and told Mother to rest easy and not to worry about a single thing.

She closed her eyes and quickly slipped back to sleep. Grandmother sat on an easy chair next to the bed and held her daughter's hand. Tears were streaming down her face, but she made no noise for fear of disturbing her daughter. Grandfather put a reassuring hand on my shoulder, as we stood watch over Mother until we were ushered away by a staff nurse, who needed to attend to Mother's observations. With heavy hearts, we left Mother to the good care of the nurses. Aunty Pam suggested that under the circumstances, I spend the night with my grandparents rather than go home to an empty house. I knew that the right thing to do was probably take her advice, after all, she is their daughter, their little girl and they too are distressed. I guess Aunty Pam was also considering her own situation, for if I was with them offering emotional support, then it left her off the hook to pursue her own interests. Truth be known, I wasn't sure what I wanted, but I did need time to think clearly and get my head straight before I went into meltdown mode. Being with my grandparents would not give me the opportunity to come to terms with how Mother's illness was about to affect my future. I made some excuse about needing to tidy the kitchen and sort out the room the lads had slept in and asked to be dropped off at home.

The first thing I noticed as I entered the house, was the lingering smell of the cooked dinner; the familiar Sunday evening smell of cold roast mutton and the tangy aroma of the mint sauce. I realised that I hadn't eaten since breakfast, so I warmed up some of the leftovers that I had plated up earlier and sat in front of the television watching the news. As usual, it was all depressing, which was not helpful at all. I changed channels and watched a repeat episode of a classic Morecombe and Wise comedy show. Even they couldn't raise a laugh from my tight lips. Unsure if I should contact Father at this late hour, I decided that perhaps tomorrow would be soon enough to tell him. Although they have been divorced for years now and theoretically she is no longer a part of his life or his responsibility in any way, I guess he would be most upset if he heard about her illness from another source. The problem is, that I'm unsure what shift he is on tomorrow and no way will I pass on the information to his orange face wife. Perhaps I will leave a message for him to ring me on my mobile. I wish Father had a mobile of his own, he bought me one and still sends me a top-up voucher every month and yet he goes without one himself.

I know for sure that I am going to struggle to sleep tonight without a little help, so I rummage through the sideboard in the hope of finding a little something to calm me down or with luck, sedate me. Eventually, right at the back of the cupboard, I find a bottle of something. Disappointingly, it is a bottle of sherry. Not exactly my favourite tipple, but it will have to do.

CHAPTER THIRTY-SEVEN

Grace's Diary

21 AUGUST 1997

I knew this day would come, my secret is out. I can no longer hide away from the truth. Alfie and my family have to know about my condition and all that it entails. My sister, Pam, will now need to help me with our parents and Paul will have to be informed, as Alfie is going to need emotional support. Of course, I have known for some time what the likely progress of the disease would be and the journey that follows, somehow, I need to prepare Alfie for the reality of my disease and what it involves. There will be no point in me sugar coating the truth. Out of all the people who love me, he is the only one likely to be able to understand the disease and prognosis. I will get through this and once I'm stable enough to go home, I will need to begin peritoneal dialysis on a regular basis. I now know that with support from the community nursing team and the renal nurses, this will be easily managed.

More importantly, I have been reassured that with time, my health and energy levels will improve. Fortunately, it is company policy to be paid the full rate of pay for three months while off sick and I plan to use this time wisely. I will be very careful with my money as there is no knowing what is around the corner. Eventually, I will need to reduce my working week down to four days so that I can take a day off midweek to recharge my batteries, which actually means I will be giving my diseased kidneys a rest whilst I undergo dialysis.

I guess with his increasing knowledge of pharmacy, Alfie will have some idea of the dialysis process and the medications I will need to take for the remainder of my life. I'm not sure whether it is an advantage or a disadvantage having a son who is knowledgeable about such things. One thing for sure is that I won't be able to pull the wool over his eyes anymore. I know that it is only a few weeks before the end of term exams and indeed the end of his first year. I don't want to put any pressure on him to spend the whole time with me, but for selfish reasons, I would very much appreciate it if he did. I can't decide if I should share my financial concerns with Alfie, it could be counterproductive in terms of his future plans and put undue pressure on him. Perhaps I will wait and take the lead from him.

CHAPTER THIRTY-EIGHT

Alfie

The past week I have visited Mother at the hospital twice a day, ensuring that she has company, at least for a couple of hours. Aunty Pam has also visited, bringing my grandparents with her. Although the car is available for me to use, I am not on Mother's insurance, so I am unable to make use of it. Perhaps we need to think about adding me as a named driver, which will be helpful in the future, as I anticipate that Mother's illness will peak and trough over time. It will likely entail further hospital visits and admissions. Although I have been studying very hard for my end of term exams, I have also been researching renal failure prognosis and treatment options. I now know that Mother has decided on peritoneal dialysis, so I have spent some time getting an understanding of the process. In addition, I have been researching the pharmacology of the drugs used for renal disease, including the monitoring and the side effects.

Although I haven't approached the subject yet, common sense tells me that she is not going to be able to continue working flat-out full-time anymore, which puts me in a dilemma. I have made contact with Stu to make enquiries, if I could crash out at their place next year. I know that I will no longer be eligible for the halls of residence and need to find some digs, so perhaps my living accommodation expenses can be reduced. In addition, I need to find myself a part-time job to fit in with my studies. Hopefully, something will crop up. Meanwhile, I have made contact with Mr Rossi, my old boss at Antico Restaurant where I used to waiter for. He was delighted to see me and was happy to employ me as a waiter in the evenings throughout the whole summer break. He inquired about Mother and said that he looks forward to catching up with all of my news. How great is that?

When I told Mother my plans, the relief on her face was a wonderful sight. She is to be discharged from the hospital at the weekend. Everything is in place at home for her peritoneal dialysis. All of the necessary equipment has been delivered and I even cleaned the house. Aunty Pam has made up Mother's bed with clean sheets and she has done all of the laundry. She is staying for a week, until Mother is up and running with the dialysis, enabling me to return to university to sit my exams.

I have studied hard this week and feel fairly confident. I have promised to return next weekend, just until Sunday evening, when I will need to return to complete the remainder of my exams. After which, I have to vacate the halls of residence. I have made arrangements with the guys to move my belongings into their place and they will take care of my stuff while I am living at home and working at Antico Restaurant during the summer break. This will be their last year at university, my second year, so I guess we will have to make the most of it.

I know that Mother is to be off from work for at least twelve weeks, during which time she is to receive full sickness benefits, which has reassured her, for now. We have spoken of the importance of maintaining her strength and the long-term implications. I have asked her to consider reducing her working week by half to enable the maintenance of her dialysis. I arranged for an independent financial advisor to visit one evening to give us advice and discovered that Mother had some kind of sickness insurance that will pay a lump sum to help with medical expenses. The mortgage on the house has been extended, resulting in a smaller monthly payment and we have switched energy suppliers and got rid of the landline, as Mother already has a mobile phone she can use instead. Overall, we have made enough savings to reassure Mother that she has nothing to worry about. I am planning to get some kind of employment to help towards my own living expenses when I return to university. I'm not sure exactly what I will do, perhaps pizza delivery or evening bar work. Either way, I need to earn hard cash and fast.

Returning to university and leaving Mother behind was difficult for me, but I know she had plenty of support. I completed the remainder of my exams and returned home to spend the holidays with Mother. Going back to the restaurant stirred up a lot of memories, some good, some painful. I faced these demons and earned the much-needed cash. I really did well with the tips and have managed to save a fair bit of money.

Mother is progressing well with the dialysis and looking stronger every day. She is getting her grit and determination back. I can see the return of her lioness spirit. After the summer break, I returned to university with great anticipation. And my fingers crossed.

Great news with my exam results. However, for some reason I have been whistled in to see the head of the department, to discuss some issues they have with the presentation of my work. I haven't mentioned this to anyone, especially not my family.

My transition from the halls of residence and into the exciting world of student digs went without a hitch as I expected, made all the easier by the fact that I've known the lads I'm sharing with for the past year. Although my room is small, it is ok. It has plenty of storage, but more importantly, the price is right and with careful financial planning, I should scrape through. My biggest issue is the shared rooms. The kitchen is always a mess, with our different schedules, there always appears to be one or the other of us cooking something and leaving dirty pots. At first, this freaked me out, but I have now come to terms with the disorganisation, provided I keep my own room in order, giving me space to return from the cluttered common room and greasy kitchen.

Mother wanted to visit me in my new digs, which is fair enough, but no way would I let her visit until I had warned the guys, so we could do a bit of a cleanup. I gave them all a pair of marigold gloves, a bucket of soapy water and bleach. To be honest, between us, we made a decent job of the place. However, when Mother arrived, the smell of bleach was a dead giveaway, but she just smiled and nodded her head saying it was a credit to us lads that we even considered using the bleach. She was grateful they had all offered their hands of friendship to her son.

Never one to visit empty handed, she provided lunch for us all. She had made a delicious homemade shepherd's pie, thick with meat and gravy. She also put some chips in the oven so there was plenty to go around. Before leaving us, Mother went to the boot of the car, she beckoned me over and pointed to the inside where there was a crate of lager.

'For you and your friends Alfie,' she hugged me tightly and told me of how much her heart swelled with love and pride for me.

When I returned her hug, I was careful not to squeeze too much, even so, I felt her wince as my arms enveloped her small frame, feeling her ribs beneath my touch. My heart felt heavy in my chest, a familiar feeling washed over me, a deep ache of emotions from the past, only now doubled in intensity. My mind swimming with visions of Mags, long hidden in my psyche, but never forgotten.

That night my sleep was disturbed, my dreams, crazy, as images of Mother, Mags and Joy were intertwined. I saw Mother as a goth, tied up to a kidney dialysis machine, smiling at me. Mags sat at the side of her with her face devoid of make-up and her hair short and spiky, she is holding Mother's hand as Joy stands behind her wearing one of Mother's aprons. I woke up wet through with sweat, shivering amongst the cold, damp bedding. I felt too weak to get out of bed and not for the first time, wished I was back at home where I only had to call out and Mother would comfort me. In my dream like state, I began to ruminate on the future, on Mother's future. If only she had allowed herself to find a new companion, maybe in time she could have fallen in love, someone to be by her side in her old age. As things stand, she has only me and Aunty Pam. My grandparents won't be around to see Mother grow old or maybe she won't grow old. Maybe her diseased kidneys will shorten her life.

I can't bear to think of my life without her, I can't bear to think of her suffering, I am getting anxious. I can feel my jaw tighten and my hands shake. I feel nauseous and it is rising up my throat. I reach my waste paper bin just in time as my body purges itself of the acidic contents of my gut. I hate being sick and find the whole process very frightening. As the vomit gathers in my throat, I feel as though I am drowning. I can't breathe. My heart is racing and my stomach is cramping and twisting itself until the whole contents have been expelled, at which point I crawl towards the bed and despite the wet sheets, climb back inside.

The curtains in my room are badly fitted, allowing a little watery light in the room which stirs me awake. The first thing I notice is the smell. I have always had a hypersensitive smell, but even someone with a poor olfactory system would gag at the stench. I recognise the sour smell of vomit mixed with body odour and sweat. I cannot stand the smell of my own body. As I try to prop myself up in bed, I notice that my arms and legs feel heavy and ache, they feel like lead weights attached to the rest of my body. Gradually I slip my legs over the edge of the bed, supporting my upper body by placing my heavy arms either side of me, pressed into the saggy mattress. I wait until the dizziness subsides and force myself to stand up. My bladder is pressing hard against my bowels sending an urgent message to my brain, but my legs don't want to respond. I call out loudly to Aaron who is in the next room.

He hears my call and enters my room. 'Christ mate, what's happened in here, it stinks to high heaven?' Aaron takes one look at me and shuts up, he puts his arms behind me, lifting me off the edge of the bed.

'Let's get you to the bathroom Alf and quick.'

I sit on the loo, lady fashion and empty the steaming wee from my overstretched bladder as Aaron fetches me a mug of water. I am shivering and shaking, so grab a towel that is on the floor. Although damp, I wrap it around my shoulders. The weight of it against my body offers a little comfort. I sit on the loo for ages until the shape of the seat is digging into my bum cheeks. A commotion outside the door brings me back to reality as the rest of the guys burst into the bathroom.

'Come on mate, we all need the loo,' jokes Jim, as he helps to pull me off the seat and immediately lifting the seat and peeing a river of wee into the stained bowl.

Stu grabs me as I stumble forward. He takes me to the sofa, puts a scatter cushion behind my head and lays a thick tartan throw over my shivering body.

'Reckon you've got flu mate. I'll get you a couple of paracetamol and a sweet tea. Looks like you will be missing your lectures today.'

In my muddled mind, I realised that was not the only thing I was going to miss. I have an appointment with the head of the department. I don't know what it is about and I am desperate to be enlightened, but there is no way I am leaving this sofa today. Stu sets up a tray on the coffee table with a jug of water, a pack of paracetamol and a half packet of digestive biscuits. Before the guys leave for university, they bring me a pot of tea and a chipped mug, give me a high five each and leave me to sleep, which is what I am still doing when Joy arrives. Apparently, Jim happened to see her on the campus and told her that it looks like I had man flu.

Joy bounced into the lounge like a small puppy dog fussing around me and talking nonstop, making constant comments about my man odour. I heard her retching as she went into my bedroom and removed the waste bin. Coming from vomit girl that's a first. I felt a smile creep across my very dry, cracked lips, as I thought of the many times in the past that I had held her hair back as she spewed out the contents of her stomach. I guess I will need a new bin. I noticed that Joy returned from the backyard without it. Half an hour later, after she had stripped my bed and opened the window to air the room, Joy came and sat with me.

'Right Alf, don't be bashful, I have filled the bath ready for you, if you need help getting in, just say the word and I'm all yours.'

I knew that my body reeked of sweat and the smell of sickness, I also guessed that I was in need of assistance. Joy is my friend, as far as I am aware, she has no romantic notions, but girls can be difficult to read and often hide their real feelings. I wasn't sure how to play this one, but with no other alternative, I had to submit and allow her to support me to the bathroom. I swear she was enjoying this. As a matter of decency, I left my boxer shorts on and allowed her to help me into the tub. It felt so good, the warm water enveloping my chilled and aching body. I lay my head against the bath and closed my heavy eyelids. Joy remained in the bathroom, I heard her rummaging through the cupboard underneath the sink.

'Alf, can I wash your hair? There are all kinds of sticky substances in it.'

Without opening my eyes, I nodded my head. She gently poured warm water over my hair and gently washed it. She massaged my scalp, paying attention to my temples. Her fingers moved in a circular movement, which felt quite soothing. There was something sensual about the way she was touching me and despite the man flu that had completely rendered my body useless, I felt myself getting aroused. I don't think that was Joys' intention and I'm sure she didn't notice. However, it made me uneasy and in unfamiliar territory. Mags had been the only one to create this feeling and crazy as it was, even to me. I felt as though I was betraying her memory.

As the water chilled, so did my arousal. Joy had managed to find one of the huge bath sheets that Mother had given me when I first came to university. She held it out for me as I climbed out of the tub and wrapped the sheet firmly around my trembling body. The effort of getting in and out of the bath wiped me out, so was very grateful when Joy helped me back to my room and into the freshly made bed. It felt like heaven, I was so grateful to Joy. The room was a little chilly, so she closed the window and left me to rest. I think I managed a couple of hours of sleep. I stirred as Joy came into my room with a tray of food. She had warmed us a bowl of soup each and must have been out to get some fresh bread rolls. Joy propped me up with some scatter cushions that she had removed from the sofa and handed me a tray. Surprisingly, I managed to finish the whole bowl. Joy handed me two paracetamols and felt my forehead.

'You will survive Alf. I will be back later on. I am so glad that finally, I have been able to help you. All of those times you have taken care of me, cleaned me up and stayed with me all night, have not been forgotten. I will always be eternally grateful to you. We are mates Alf; soul mates.

'Now we both need to push hard and complete our degree. Me because my Father had such great hopes for me and I want to make sure that I prove to the woman who gave birth to me that I am my father's daughter and his memory will be a lasting legacy through me. You, Alf, are destined for great things. Make your mother proud.'

CHAPTER THIRTY-NINE

Grace's Diary

SEPTEMBER 1997

I couldn't rest until I had seen Alfie's new place. I realise he was only allowed to stay in the halls of residence for the first year, a good introduction to student life, especially as the kitchen and common rooms were cleaned by the domestic staff. When he was in the halls I felt reassured that they all looked out for each other. Now I am not so sure. I know the guys he lives with are all his friends; sensible lads studying law. Yet I have this niggling worry that he could be led astray. Alfie is so vulnerable and doesn't always make sensible choices.

Mags was a lovely girl and from what I have been told, so is Joy. However, I can't help thinking that Alfie seems to be attracted to girls who hold deep secrets within them. Girls who need saving in one way or another. I think Alfie feels the need to be a saviour; he certainly seems to attract needy people. He looked a little peaky when I left him, very pale and quiet. I hope he isn't coming down with anything. I keep meaning to ask the consultant if my kidney disease is a genetic disorder, but perhaps subconsciously this is deliberate and I don't want to know the truth? Either way, it is out of my hands.

Alfie has passed all of his first-year exams, although he still hasn't provided me with much information. I'm not quite sure why he usually loves going into great detail about each subject area. Perhaps he is tired. Either way, he will talk to me when he is ready. He seems to be enjoying the course content and has no plans to change direction. Apparently, some students change course after the first year having realised they had made a mistake, but Alfie seems settled. Long may it last?

CHAPTER FORTY

Alfie

It took me a whole week of rest and rehabilitation before I felt strong enough to attend my first lecture. Joy had kept me up to date with the subject area and shared her notes with me. We are currently studying the modes of action of drugs at the cellular level. I am totally fascinated with every aspect of pharmacology and have never had any doubts as to my future career. I have had a reminder letter to see the head of the year, so have made an appointment for this afternoon. I am still unsure what it is all about, but I will soon find out.

Well, that was a surprise. Apparently, some of the faculty have reported concerns about my inability to take notes during class and the state of my writing. They seem to think that I am not taking the course seriously, as I am annoying them with my constant fidgeting in class. Where did that come from? It appears that the exam papers were assessed by an outside source and although the content and the answers were mostly correct, a complaint was made about the standard of my writing. Well, now I am really annoyed. I have been referred to an educational psychologist.

Spiralling, negative thoughts fill my mind. What if the faculty think that I am not suitable to continue into my second year? I have never had a plan B in terms of a career choice and I have no intention of changing to an alternate degree programme. The appointment with the psychologist is not for another two weeks. Meanwhile, I continue to attend my lectures with Joy, but feel somehow detached from the process. This does not go unnoticed by some of the other students in my group, who occasionally join me and Joy in the refectory, where we sometimes sit for lunch.

Some of the guys are really nosy, always wanting to interfere in other people's lives. I think they are expecting me to quit the course. We have already lost a third of the students who didn't pass their first-year exams and I can see the remaining students forming little clicks of like-minded people. Occasionally we need to work in groups, particularly when we have a specific project to work on. Generally, I just get on with the task at hand and avoid small talk, which the others appear to thrive on.

I'm struggling to concentrate on my work and the problem is reinforced by my lack of sleep. It takes me ages to drop off to sleep and I usually only manage a couple of hours before I wake up again in a blind panic from the all-consuming dreams that plague me every night. After a full week of sleep deprivation, I finally succumb to Aaron's suggestion of self-help in the form of drinking myself into oblivion until my body shuts down. This actually works, but leaves me feeling totally hungover all day. Not to mention the amount of cash this consumes from my dwindling finances.

Finally, the day of my appointment arrives and with great trepidation, I walk into the lion's den - Professor Thompson's consulting room. I am pleasantly surprised at the relaxed layout of the room, the professor offers me his hand to shake, which I take and am rewarded with a firm handshake and a welcoming smile, immediately putting me at ease.

'So, Alfie. Do you understand the reason for this appointment?'

I shake my head as for some strange reason, I find that I have suddenly become speechless.

'No worries,' he says as he directs me over to an easy chair, placed by the side of a coffee table which is piled high with folders and documents. He pulls over another chair and sits squarely opposite me.

'The thing is, Alfie, your tutors have been concerned about you for some time, but there is no question of your level of intelligence or your suitability for the pharmacology course. It is more about their observations in terms of your social interactions and flexibility of thought. More recently, it has been reported that although you can reel off appropriate information verbatim, the standard and quality of your written work is quite untidy. I would like to explore the reasons behind these problems and see if we can help you, how does that sound?'

The word help sounded very good indeed, enabling me to feel a little more relaxed. Over coffee, he enquired about my childhood, asking me to explain about my early years at school and about my family dynamics. He was recording the entire consultation, something that he had requested permission to do. When he enquired about my social interaction with the opposite sex, the professor began to look uncomfortable.

I felt sorry for him, so I made the whole process easy, by informing him that I only had interest in females. He wanted to know very personal details, managing to coax out of me information about my relationship with Mags that I have never ever spoken aloud before. He appeared very understanding and empathetic. At the end of the session, the professor said that he would like to see me again the following week and perform some kind of psychometric tests on me if I was in agreement. It sounded satisfactory to me, so a further appointment was arranged.

I was rather hoping that now I was more aware of the reasons that I had been referred to the psychology department, perhaps I might manage to have a more restful night, but that wasn't the case. I was wide awake and walking around the kitchen at four o'clock in the morning. Steve's brother, Chris, was sleeping on the sofa in the lounge, he was visiting for a week and was well aware of my poor sleep pattern. I guess I woke him up again when I visited the kitchen for the fifth time that night. He didn't look very happy with me. Chris pressed something into my hand.

'Here mate, take this Valium, I'm sick of hearing you pace up and down, night after night. No need to thank me, just go back to bed.'

Of course, I am well aware of what Valium does, but what harm could one ten milligram tablet do? I grabbed a glass of water and swallowed the tablet, hoping for a speedy effect. Which is exactly what happened and I had the best sleep that I have had in months, with no hangover symptoms the following day.

I felt so refreshed and ready to face the day. Joy was as observant as ever and remarked that at last, the Alf that she knew had re-emerged, however, it was short-lived as I began to appreciate it was a temporary benefit only and the following night I was pacing the floor again. Chris was leaving the next day so in desperation, I asked if he could spare me another Valium. However, this time there was a price to pay. He sold me fourteen tablets for £20.00, which I readily agreed to.

All of my life I have struggled with sleep. Not as bad as these past few weeks, or as I like to call it, *the pre-chemical weeks*. I re-play things in my head and internalise how others react to me. My dreams have always been of a sensational nature and often with intrusive thoughts. The Valium changed all of that and I began to realise how good it feels to have all of that noise out of my head.

My next appointment with Professor Thompson, for me, was a completely different consultation from the first occasion. This time I felt totally in control. Which did not escape his astute observations of me. In fact, within the first five minutes, he remarked that I appeared unusually relaxed. I guess he had his own suspicions that I was self-medicating, but chose not to raise the subject. Instead, he continued to ask about my childhood and about my days at school. Then I was asked to perform a number of psychometric tests, which were actually very interesting and I could see where it was all leading. Arrangements were once again made for the following week when the professor planned to evaluate his assessments and provide a written report for the faculty. He reassured me, that I was to be given an explanation of the report.

My life was feeling good. The guys were noticing the subtle changes in me, as I allowed myself to chill out with them in the evenings, playing cards or watching movies. Sometimes Joy came around to our place and sat with us on the dog-eared sofa. She too mentioned that at last, I seemed to be chilling out. The problem for me was the dwindling supply of Valium and I had no idea how to get more, not without making contact with my original supplier. I tried to take them on alternate nights in order to make them last. However, on the nights I omitted them, I was unable to sleep at all and felt more agitated than ever. I had no idea how to contact Chris, other than to ask Steve for his number, which would arouse his suspicions.

Somehow, I needed to find a way round this, before I got agitated again. Fortunately for me, Steve did not care where he left his mobile phone. So, one evening, whilst he was in the shower, I took the opportunity to enter his room and search amongst the vast piles of his belongings scattered about his floor. How low I had stooped, entering my friend's room and stealing his mobile phone. Of course, I was planning to return the phone, once I had retrieved his brother's number. Once in the safety of my own room, it didn't take me long to locate Chris's number and jot it down, with plans to ring him later. Getting the mobile phone back where I found it was a little tricky, so in the end, I stuffed it down the sofa, with plans to suggest such a place to Steve when he complained about his missing phone. He had left it switched on, so eventually, he was sure to find it. Especially if some obliging friend rang the number.

Around ten o'clock, I told the lads that I was going to the union bar for a drink with Joy. My lies are getting the better of me, but needs must and it's not as if I haven't lied before. What's one more going to matter?

Chris was very obliging, for a large fee, which was definitely going to put me in the red. No matter, I guess I will find some means of making a bit of money on the side. Meanwhile, I am guaranteed a few more good night's sleep and relaxing days, free from my overactive mind. I understand the mode of action of the Valium and I am well aware of its addictive properties, but I am sure that I can keep this under control. I have been taught about how the benzodiazepine drugs help with anxiety and panic attacks. Everything that I have been told reinforces the evidence of how the drug works on the GABA neurotransmitter in the brain. It certainly slows down my overactive, crazy mind. Maybe I will just take it on alternate days so that I am in control of the substance and not the other way around. I guess that we all need a little help from time to time and mine comes in the form of synthetic chemicals. It's not as if I'm smoking dope or self-medicating by getting myself wasted on alcohol like most of the guys here. Besides, I have an important appointment with Professor Thompson in two days' time and maybe he has some good news for me. Perhaps I can join Mensa, who knows?

CHAPTER FORTY-ONE

Grace's Diary

12 NOVEMBER 1997

I have to admit, I am very relieved to discover that my kidney disease is definitely not a genetic disorder and my precious Alfie will not be affected. He has not been aware of my concerns, after all, he has enough to worry about with his studies. Now in his second year and it all seems to be going well. I had my reservations at first when he moved out of halls, but I'm coming to understand student life a little more, at least I think I am. I have heard such shocking stories about what some of the students get up to at university, but I know my son, he will not let me down. After all, to my knowledge he has had two very bad experiences in the past and hopefully he has learned from them.

Recently, my health has deteriorated further and it is only a matter of time before I need to attend the hospital for dialysis. The last renal biopsy shows that I have stage four chronic kidney disease, meaning treatment with haemodialysis is imminent. Soon, very soon, I will need to finish work. I have been led to believe that I can claim some kind of sickness benefit, although I will need to look into this. I am so glad that my parents encouraged me to take out an insurance policy when I first started work, this will be very useful if I need to cash it in. Thankfully, I think that I have enough saved to cover the cost of the tuition fees which will help Alfie complete his second year of studies, but after that, we will need some help with finances. Perhaps Alfie can get a part-time job and maybe he could speak to his father.

I have been told that sometimes the miners' union help families with educational needs. Last week, Hazel told me that one of the fifth form lads in her youngest son's class had been given money from a special fund set aside for members and their families, by the National Union of Mineworkers. He had been given enough to purchase the much-needed revision books he required. It would be such a relief if they would sponsor Alfie in some way. I'm not sure about such things so I will have to research the possibilities. Maybe I will ring Alfie next week and suggest he comes home for a few days over the Christmas holidays so that I can have a serious talk with him about both of our futures.

CHAPTER FORTY-TWO

Alfie

I'm sat in Professor Thomson's consulting room waiting for him to look up from the case notes he is reading. This is unusual behaviour for him. Previously, he has made eye contact with me within seconds of my entry into the room, which generally makes me feel awkward and uncomfortable. Actually, it could be a blessing in disguise, for I fear that guilt is written all over my face. I have this crazy idea, that because he is a professor of psychology, he can read my mind. Or take one look at my face and just know, beyond any doubt, that I am taking benzo drugs.

I can't help wondering if I am getting paranoid? I've read about this and a number of other mental health problems. Apparently, mental health problems are more prevalent amongst males and the statistics suggest it is on the rise. It appears to be a subject that most adults try to avoid talking about and the National Health Service does not invest in, with equal parity. Some would argue that it is the Cinderella service of the NHS. I have been reading more psychology books these past few weeks than the pharmacology books that I should be reading. Mags would be proud of me. I have this niggly suspicion the professor feels uncomfortable about the report in front of him. The silence in the room is deafening and I swear that the tick of the clock on his desk, is getting louder. I wish his phone would ring or his secretary run into the room and shout, 'Fire! Fire! Fire! Evacuate the building.'

Finally, he looks up, adjusts his reading glasses and smooths his floppy grey hair back from his forehead. I notice a fine layer of perspiration forming above his upper lip and his mouth tightens as though he is about to say something distasteful.

'So, young man. I have read the results of the tests that you performed on your last visit and have collated all of the information you gave me about yourself. These consultations have revealed a number of interesting facts, along with my own personal observations, gained from our social interactions and conversation. As you know, I am one of a team of educational psychologists here at the university and we regularly have case conference meetings to discuss diagnosis and management.'

This is getting heavy for me and I can see him dithering. I look straight through him and surprise myself with my directness.

'Sounds serious, Proff. Have I got long to live?'

'Have you covered any modules related to brain biology and function Alfie? Or psychology?' he replies in response.

I nod my head and tell him that it just so happens that I have recently taken an interest in that area of science and I am finding it fascinating.

'Well, that makes my job a little easier,' he replies. 'You see, Alfie, your symptoms suggest a diagnosis of Asperger syndrome. To be more precise, you appear to have a neurobiological disorder, which is part of the autistic spectrum. As yet, the cause is unknown, but we suspect a possibility of it being an inherited trait. Having spent some time with you, I have observed that you are a clever young man. In fact, your results show that you have a high level of intelligence, with less than average social skills and a tendency towards obsessive behaviour and quite likely, obsessive thoughts.

'My main concern is your impulsivity and potential risk-taking behaviour Alfie. Although we know very little about this condition, what we do know is that it is not about the traits that you display, it is more about the traits that you have lost. It is a neurological disorder. The majority of people are neurotypical. Think of yourself as though a part of your brain is neurotypical, but another part is not quite wired up in the correct sequence.

'Did you know, Alfie, that some of the greatest people of our times likely displayed similar symptoms to you? For example, we think that Albert Einstein and Mozart were likely autistic.'

Well, I wasn't expecting that. I stare at Professor Thompson as though he has just spoken to me in a foreign language. The Valium I took earlier is beginning to take effect. I sit there in front of the professor with a blank expression on my face. I feel as though I am not in the room, but looking through a window at myself. I know that I should be affected by his words, but the drugs have rendered my mind numb, in fact, I almost feel nothing, no emotion, no pain, no feeling. I want to lay my head down on the desk in front of me and go to sleep forever.

Did he say Asperger syndrome? I vaguely remember either reading or hearing, that word somewhere before.

'Alfie, did you hear what I have just said, do you understand?'

Somehow, I manage to respond. I stand up to leave and as I reach the door, Professor Thompson calls out to me and informs me that one of the team will be paying me a home visit to sit and discuss how they can help me.

I don't remember making my way back to the digs, but I obviously managed to make it to the sofa, for I was rudely awaken from my stupor when Steve came back and sat on me for a lark.

'Hey buddy, what you are doing lolling on the couch? It's not like you, I reckon you must have that post-viral thing that happens after man flu. My mate came down with that, took him weeks to get back on track.'

Without realising, Steve had given me the best excuse ever for my recent behaviour. Mother has insisted that I should visit her next week and if anyone can suss me out, she can. So, now I have a tailor-made excuse.

Joy accompanied me most days to class and occasionally we were paired up to work on a project together. Since my brain has calmed down, it takes longer to retrieve past knowledge. Although this is comforting on one level. I find it annoying that I have lost my edge, lost the sharpness of mind and the ability to process new information at the same rate as I did before taking my increasing doses of Valium.

She is asking questions and enquired if I have started smoking weed.

Of course, I strongly denied that accusation, which was easy enough to do, considering it was a truthful reply. Fed up with her intrusive questioning I told Joy that I was most definitely suffering from a post-viral syndrome which may go on for weeks. Clever move on my part, this gives me a great cover story, by which time I plan to wean myself off the Valium.

That evening Joy came to my room, full of enthusiasm and a pile of books in her hand. For two hours, I sat with her on my crumpled bed discussing acquired and passive immunity. I watched with interest as her face lit up while we debated the virtues of the vaccination programme providing active immunity against serious microbial disease. Joy did not want to leave and I must admit she had fired up my brain and for the first time in weeks, my interest in pharmacology was reinforced. We sat chatting until the early hours of the morning, studying the cellular immune response and the humoral response.

The withdrawal symptoms from the Valium were creeping up on me and I was feeling a little twitchy, but somehow, I was able to compensate by allowing Joy to distract me with her unending enthusiasm. I persuaded her to leave around two a.m., in fact, I practically had to pull her off the bed. I got the impression that she was wanting to spend the night with me and for that, I was flattered. She must think it very odd that I did not jump at the chance to enjoy a night of rampant sex with her. I was tempted, oh yes, very tempted and my body betrayed the message loud and clear, something Joy had clearly observed. My body was willing and able, but my mind was sinking fast and I needed to take a tablet. She finally accepted my poor excuse that I did not want to ruin our friendship as I valued her as a good friend and not a friend with benefits.

Taking the Valium as late as I did, would have a knock-on effect the next day. I tried to reason with myself, that I didn't need to take one and I could ride out the withdrawal symptoms that were making me feel anxious and nauseous. For a while, I tried to concentrate on thinking of distraction methods that would take my mind off the Valium. However, the chemical won the battle and as I finally lay on my bed with my mind anaesthetised by the GABA, I drifted off to sleep.

The rest of the week drags. Twice I try to delay taking the tablets; twice I try to reduce the dose and twice I failed. I have contacted Chris, whose number I now have in my directory, on speed dial. The week drags and I am counting the days until my rendezvous with him. We have arranged to meet outside of the railway station. He knows what I want. I have the £20 and just enough cash left for my train ticket, then I am completely wiped out. Not a penny to my name. I hate to do this, but I have no alternative than to ask Mother for a loan. Chris is not at the designated meeting point. After phoning him three times, he finally answers his mobile.

'I'm on my way dude, don't panic. I will be there in ten minutes.'

Sure enough, in the distance, I see him swaggering along. He is wearing the latest in fashionable men's wear, including a top-of-the-range black leather bomber jacket that I guess is proper Italian leather. He looked as though he had not a care in the world with his smug expression, which was beginning to wind me up big time. I have missed my train and let Mother down. The next one is in two hours, by which time any food that she is likely to have prepared, will be ruined.

Chris is unapologetic. He hands me a package and asks for £50.00. I tell him there must be some mistake as the last time he charged me £20.00. He fobs me off with some excuse about the difficulty in obtaining them and his supplier has upped the price.

'Out of my hands mate.' As he holds his hands up in the air.

I know I'm being duped. He knows my desperation, after all, he started me on this path and now he is leading me all the way down it. I ask him for £20.00 worth, for that is all that I have got. He winks at me and gives me the package.

'You owe me now dude, so when I come calling I expect to be paid in one way or another.'

With that, he nonchalantly walks away, hands in his pockets, head in the air. I stand for a while watching him as he walks into the distance. His broad back and shoulders, making him stand out in the crowd of people leaving the station. I feel an overwhelming sense of dread; a black cloud of anguish weighs heavy on my conscience. Although this was a brief feeling, no more than a minute, it feels like a lifetime. I have nearly two hours to sit around waiting for the next train. The station is freezing cold and I swear it is just like a wind tunnel as the cold air whips around my head. I wish that I had a hood on my jacket or at least a scarf around my neck. I need to get my act together, instead of obsessing about my next dose of Valium

FORTY-THREE

Grace's Diary

7 DECEMBER 1997

Alfie is coming home for Christmas; I am so excited. We have made plans to meet up with family and friends so I thought it would be a good idea to go shopping for some new clothes.

I asked Hazel to come with me so that we could make it a girly day out. I was worried that the shopping might take it out of me. However, Hazel was very considerate and she drove us to Nottingham city centre. I haven't been shopping in the city for a very long time and I forgot that how much better it was than our nearest town. I felt like a child in a sweet shop, however, I had to be careful with money.

Every so often, Hazel suggested that we should take a break and we would rest on a bench or sometimes have a drink in a café. I enjoyed watching everyone do their Christmas shopping. The atmosphere felt magical and I even saw a few snowflakes gently falling onto the ground. It reminded me of when I was pregnant with Alfie. I felt really happy.

We went to Debenhams department store and I went into the changing room to try on some festive dresses. Oh, good lord. It was horrific. As I looked into the full-length mirror I was shocked at what I saw. I was nothing but skin and bone. My skin a sallow shade of yellow and my eyes tired and puffy. I tried on a size eight dress, but it was actually too big, anyhow, when I saw the price tag I realised that it was well out of my budget.

I told Hazel that I had to be careful with money, so we went to a charity shop instead and I found a little, black dress in a size six which was perfect. I spotted a large pair of Jackie Onassis sunglasses, that all the stars seem to get away with it, under the umbrella of being stylish. I wondered if I could hide behind a pair, but it would probably be a step too far for me. Still, it will be something to consider in the summer.

Hazel treated me to lunch, saying it was my Christmas present. We went to a restaurant on Bridlesmith Gate called Café Rouge and it was fabulous. I loved the French décor and the food was delicious. However, Hazel then shocked me. She said she didn't want to ruin the day, but she felt it was time she confessed something. I was rather intrigued at first and then she told me that she had kept something important from me for years. She admitted that one of the reasons she befriended me was because she had heard about Paul's affair and she knew I would need a friend. She said she felt disgusted by what he was doing and she was concerned for me. She could never bring herself to be the one to tell me what was going on though. I thought she was going to tell me a bigger secret than that. I always suspected she wanted to tell me something, but I had wrongly thought it was about Alfie. Back then everybody in the village gossiped about Alfie being 'different' and I thought she wanted to discuss that. We hugged, cried, and I forgave her. After her confession, I could see she finally had some kind of absolution and I was happy for her.

Although Paul broke my heart, I have moved on now and when I get better I may even consider going on a date. Pam has managed to meet a potential husband, despite suffering intense grief, so there is every possibility it can happen to me. I will become a new woman. It will be my time soon. I know it.

9 DECEMBER 1997

I still feel exhausted from the day out in Nottingham. I can't understand it at all. I am struggling to stay awake during the day, so I feel that I have no other choice than to take afternoon naps. In fact, afternoon naps have become a ritual these past few weeks. My kidneys are struggling along on reduced capacity, dragging the rest of my body down. My internal deterioration is nothing compared to the way I look. Even that little black dress and my old Clinique make-up don't hide my illness.

I am feeling anxious about money. I didn't spend much in Nottingham, however, being off sick is an almighty blow to my already dwindling savings. My three months of sickness benefit has come to an end. My last wage packet was at the end of November. Not a good time, pre-Christmas. Sadly, I have given in my notice. It is no good to keep fooling myself into thinking that next week I will feel stronger, when in fact it is the opposite of how I am progressing. I feel so guilty being off sick and remaining on the books.

Whilst still theoretically employed, my boss and the staff are a man down, they have struggled on in the hope that I will recover enough to return. I had also hoped for this, but now I realise that it was unrealistic of me. Now I have done this, they can advertise my job. Strangely, this has taken a weight off my mind, for I have been living in dread of having to make the decision of leaving a job that I truly enjoy. Having studied and worked so hard to get it, I feel sort of empty and adrift. It is going to hit Alfie and I both very hard in different ways. I need to ensure that he completes his degree without taking on a student loan and all the responsibility that entails. Alfie will find having a large debt distracting, it will play on his mind and ultimately become another thing for him to obsess about.

I have delved deep inside my mind to think of a way around this. I have met with a mortgage advisor and have been given a little breathing space at the expense of adding further years to the terms of the mortgage, but needs must. The utility bills are bound to increase as I will be spending more time at home. Sadly, my car will have to go. The MOT, tax, and insurance are due in two months' time and I am unable to work at the moment, so as far as I'm concerned it will be an unnecessary drain on my limited income. I can arrange hospital transport to attend the dialysis sessions and maybe, Paul can help Alfie out from time to time. In fact, Paul has been helping a lot, much to his wife's annoyance. I think she is getting jealous, serves her right. Almost a taste of her own medicine! He calls round and checks in on me, however, we are just good friends now. I have no romantic feelings for Paul anymore. Susan popped by the other day, she said they had their work Christmas party at Antico Restaurant and Mr Rossi or Antonio as she called him was asking about me. I am sure he is just being friendly because he has always thought so highly of Alfie. However, when I am better, it would be nice to have a coffee with Antonio, he is a very kind man.

13 DECEMBER 1997

I am in shock. I have been so looking forward to Alfie coming home, however, it has been a nightmare. What was he thinking? Why, oh why do you have to break my heart sweet boy? I have sacrificed so much for you and my poor heart can't take it.

Last night, I was expecting Alfie to call me around 6.00 p.m. informing me of his expected time of arrival so that I could meet him at the railway station. However, two hours later he had not rung. It was unusual for Alfie to be so late without warning me. What I found most concerning was the fact that his mobile was switched off and had been for over an hour.

I made myself a small cup of weak coffee, hoping this would help to keep me awake. It failed miserably and I woke forty minutes later to the shrill sound of the telephone ringing close to my ear. I must have fallen asleep on the sofa, close to the occasional table where the phone is placed.

I answered with a tired, slurred voice. Even I thought I sounded as though I had suffered a stroke and lost my power of speech.

'Mother, is that you?' he said.

I concentrated on my breathing, forming the correct words to reassure Alfie. The last thing I wanted was to worry him more than necessary.

I clearly remember saying to Alfie, 'Where are you son? I've been really worried about you, why are you so late?'

He told me that there were delays with the trains and he asked me to meet him at the station in fifteen minutes.

So, I went to the station and stood alone on the platform. The cold wind blowing harshly causing me to struggle to remain standing against its force; my frame now so fragile that I could have easily been blown away by the next big gust. I was feeling the cold so much more recently. I had put a super thick cardigan over my dress, a bit of extra padding to fill out my emaciated body. That way, Alfie wouldn't notice.

I could see the train headlight in the distance before I heard the click-clack on the tracks. There was no mention of the train or any other train being delayed on the overhead monitor. For a moment I thought why is that? Whatever the reason, I was just happy to be spending this short time with Alfie, even though I feared that it would be stressful and less than satisfactory for him. I intended to tell him the full details of my declining health and the proposed management of the condition.

As the train pulled alongside the platform, I searched amongst the commuters eagerly standing at the doors, waiting for the green light to release the door. A number of people left the front carriages. Then I saw my Alfie. Immediately I sensed a change in him. Usually, he is bouncing off the walls with zest and energy, but tonight he walked slowly and calmly with a controlled gait as if he was concentrating on every step he made. There was no bounce in his step and no light in his eyes.

With a mighty effort, I made my way towards him. He slowly raised his right arm in gesture and gave me a lopsided smile. A false smile and I saw right through it. This was my son walking towards me, that I was sure of, but this was only the shell of my child, he looked blank. He was there in body, he looked animated, but puppet-like, as though a light has been switched off inside.

I wrapped my arms around him, squeezing him tightly, trying to send what little spirit I had left inside of me, willing it to enter his young body and light him back up. I felt him shudder as he drew away from my hold, forcing a gap between us and placing his arms on my shoulders. That was the moment I saw it, the exact moment that I recognised the faraway look in his eyes. His pupils were dark and dilated. His eyes wide open, but he did not see. I motioned for him to follow me to the car. What a pair we must have looked. Me, frail and yellow skinned. Alfie, lumbering behind me as though his feet were made of clay.

We drove home in silence, Alfie appeared to be drowsy and I fooled myself into believing it could just be pure exhaustion. I was avoiding the worst thought to take root in my mind, the one that was nagging at the very core of my conscience. Had he unwittingly or knowingly, taken a substance that was responsible for his current state? Whatever the reason, then, was not the time to address this difficult subject. I needed to prepare myself for the task ahead. Should I have dealt with the issue of Alfie potentially using drugs or should I have discussed my own health issues? Either way, both of those subjects needed to be dealt with before he returned to university.

I performed the age-old British ritual of making a pot of tea, then beckoned Alfie to join me at the table. He seemed a little more responsive, less stupefied and more alert. I wanted to hug him, make him feel my love and to draw out his pain. I reached for his hand, placing it in my own, the warmth radiated between us.

He told me that I look tired and then he bowed his head as if he could not bear to look at me any further. I wondered if I was so repulsive to look at or if he could not bear to acknowledge the way this illness has stripped me of any beauty that he might once have seen. I recognised how difficult it must be for a child to see a parent grow old and sick, it is a reminder of the fragility of the human body and our own mortality.

He surprised me and told me he was sorry. I thought that I best to tread carefully as he looked fragile. I gently asked him, 'What are you sorry for my love?'

Alfie let go of my hand and rested his head on the table. Then he confessed.

Oh, my sweet boy, you always seem to have secrets hidden in the depth of your complicated mind.

He told me that for months he had been unable to sleep due to the stress of his studies and the constant noise in his head. His tics had been increasing in severity and his obsessive thoughts incapacitated him until he was unable to endure it any longer. What he said next broke my heart.

'I know that I am different, Mother. I see, hear, and feel the world differently to others. However, I am not the only one.'

Alfie then explained to me that one of his university professors had diagnosed him as having Asperger syndrome, which is a form of autism. Through my job I have learnt a little about Asperger's and my friends Susan and Hazel have mentioned it before. Well, modern medicine has a name for my son's behaviour. I don't care what medical name is given, he is my Alfie and I will love him unconditionally, forever.

I am, however, very scared as he is self-medicating to calm his brain. He told me how the medication helped at first, but he needed more to achieve a level of peace in his mind. I tried very hard to listen calmly as he told me about his source and how he was now in Chris' debt and he feared that he had fallen into his clutches. I could well imagine what Chris had planned for my son, knowing him to be vulnerable, he was likely to engage him in the art of dealing drugs to pay for his own habit. I wonder if Alfie's Asperger's causes him to seek self-medication?

Oh, Alfie. Why? Why didn't you talk to me? I feel guilty for being caught up in my own health problems. I thought he was doing fine, I thought he was doing great. Have I taught my son this, to be secretive? I hid my poor health from him and he has been hiding his mental health problems from me. He lies. I lie. Like mother, like son. We have kept our secrets tight to our chests.

I gently told Alfie that he had nothing to be sorry for and that we can overcome this together. I suggested that he took a rest upstairs in his bedroom while I prepared the evening meal. The truth was that I felt exhausted beyond belief and desperately needed to rest. Alfie nodded in agreement and made his way upstairs.

I am now laying on the sofa, furiously scribbling away these thoughts and feelings that are spinning around in my head. If I don't write this down, I will probably go crazy. What am I going to do? How can I absolve the part that I have played? One thing is for certain, we both need help.

CHAPTER FORTY-FOUR

Alfie

Why oh, why was I so stupid to take the drug as soon as I had a supply in my hand? How could I be so weak-minded? I am pathetic. The worst of it is, that Mother knows. At least, she knows enough. There was something different about that last tablet. It looked the same, was the same shape, colour, and size, but the effect was kind of unusual. The speed of action was quite rapid and I guess my blood level was raised pretty damn quick. I can feel the effects wearing off, causing me to feel jittery with anxiety and the obsessive thoughts are creeping through the back door of my mind.

As I lay here, staring up at the ceiling in my old bedroom, looking at the familiar central light fitting, the lampshade with trains in the pattern, it occurs to me that my room has not been changed for years. So many memories come flooding back, tearing through my mind, racing faster and faster like a train speeding towards its destination. I can almost hear the blood rushing through my head.

As my heart rate gains speed, it catches up with my thought processes. Memories of Mags and I, laying on this bed, discussing philosophy flash before me like an old sepia flicker movie. I feel hot and restless, tossing and turning, causing the old spring mattress to feel the strain. I guess that's what draws Mother's attention, she must have heard the squeaky mattress downstairs.

The walls are so thin and the floorboards uneven, they are squeakier than the mattress. My thoughts change direction as it occurs to me that Mother has made no changes or improvement to the house in the years I have been away. If anything, the house is looking shabby and run down. Come to think of it, Mother is not looking so good either. Despite trying to disguise it with that ridiculously thick cardigan, her weight-loss is obvious, in fact, she looks seriously unwell.

Pressure begins to build up behind my eyes and my head feels as though it is being squeezed in a vice. I hear a tip-tapping on my bedroom door. It gets louder and louder, the sound annoying and grating on my ears.

Mother comes into my room without my say so. She walks in slowly as though every step is a great effort for her. She gently touches my forehead, just as she did when I was a child.

Her love and devotion to me, is without question. It is written on her face, in the touch of her hands, in every action she makes. I know that I am the main focus of her life, she has made many sacrifices for me. Yet here I am about to cause her more grief. God knows she doesn't deserve it and I should try and show some appreciation, make her proud, prove that her years of love and sacrifice have not been in vain. I force my eyes open and attempt a smile.

Subconsciously I make a pact with myself that I will not take any more of the drugs that are stashed away inside of my rucksack.

'Hi Alfie, are you ready for supper?' she asks in a sing-song voice that does not match her expression. 'I've made your favourite, shepherd's pie with an extra shepherd on the side.'

Mother laughs at her own joke. She is trying to keep the mood light and so I go along with the pretence even though I have no appetite.

We sit at the old kitchen table facing each other, me picking at my food and her pushing hers around the plate. I feel wired up and nauseous, withdrawal symptoms raging through my body, creating chains that I fear will trap me forever. I distract myself for a short while by focusing on Mother. I mean really paying attention to her. Here I am feeling sorry for myself when my own parent looks worse than I do.

Despite her best efforts to disguise the weight-loss, it is clear to see the thin frame beneath her clothes. She keeps fiddling with her left arm, that is why I notice the bulge beneath her sleeve. Then it dawns on me and the reality makes me feel ashamed. Not once in the past few weeks have I enquired about her health or happiness. I have been so wrapped up in my own misery that I have neglected to notice that her kidney disease has progressed and by the look of things much quicker than expected.

I point to Mother's arm and enquire if the fistula is giving her any discomfort.

Mother hesitates for a brief moment. 'Yes, Alfie. I need to talk to you about that. In fact, I fear that I have put it off for long enough probably due to my own denial. The truth is that I didn't want to worry you, what with your exams and everything. I start dialysis next week.'

I push my plate away and go to her side. She is trembling now and tears are forming in her eyes. I feel so helpless. I reach for her hand and enquire if there is anything I can do to help?

'I need you to be brave Alfie, it is imperative that you complete your degree. The one thing that you can do for me, is reassure me that you will continue with your studies. Secure a future for yourself, that way I can go to my treatments with the knowledge that this disease is not holding you back. Promise me, Alfie. Please, promise me.'

I answer with my heart, I answer yes. I promise to do as she asks, but my head is racing towards the next tablet, just the one to help me get through the night.

I help to clear away the supper pots, then sit for a while watching the television. I am counting the minutes before I can go upstairs and help myself to some relief. The BBC news channel is on and as usual, the messages are all of doom and gloom. Why is that? Why do we need to see the misery and pain of people in other countries? Don't we have enough misery of our own? Just for once, it would be nice to hear about the positive side of life. News that lifts the spirits.

I swap channels, only to listen to politicians arguing like school children and these are the people we elect to run our country. My misery deepens and my overactive mind spins out of control. Out of the blue, my mouth takes on a life of its own. I start to chant numbers, quietly at first, between pursed lips, then gradually louder until I have reached sixty. Mother is staring at me, she looks horrified, yet I continue to mutter all kinds of nonsense. When I can take no more of my mind playing tricks I race upstairs, I guess that my brain is having some kind of crazy game with me. In my room is the rucksack. Frantically I tip it upside down and shake it until the container of pills rattles to the floor, by which time I am sweating and shaking uncontrollably. My tics are nothing compared to the jerking of my body that is taking place now.

I open the container and shake a tablet into my hand. At least half a dozen falls into my palm, then I feel her. I feel Mother's arm on my shoulder.

'No Alfie, no please don't,' she says in a trembling voice.

She takes the pills from me and removes one, placing the others in the container which she slips into her dress pocket. Mother breaks the pill in half, hands half to me and checks her watch. 'Six hours Alfie, then you can have the other half. Then tomorrow it will be a quarter. I will take care of the tablets.'

Panic rises in the form of hot bile burning my throat. I take the half dose, anything to stop this torment, then I lay on the bed until my mind is once again quiet. The relief is welcome. In my lucid moments, the truth dawns on me, I have become dependent on the drugs. Chris has drawn me in and I have allowed it to happen. The first night he gave me the Valium I should have known. With my knowledge of pharmacology, how could I have been so stupid? Now I am in his debt with no way of paying him back. I am trapped. Chris was likely planning for me to join his gang of drug pushers as a way of paying him back and getting more supplies.

Mother stays with me all night. She has dragged a chair into the room and covered herself with an old afghan blanket that I had as a child. She is asleep now; her breathing sounds raspy and laboured. I don't like the sound of it at all.

With a mighty effort, I get out of bed, slowly walk over to her and gently shake her. Softly I call her name. There is no response; not a flicker of movement. What have I done? The paramedics arrive within minutes of my phone call. They ask me all kinds of questions. My mind is still in a muddle and I can't think clearly, but I answer the best that I can.

With the blue light flashing, we head off to the hospital. On the way, I realise that the Valium tablets are still in Mother's dress pocket. I cannot get hold of them without arousing suspicion, I will have to wait for an appropriate moment. Everything happens quickly once we are in the ambulance. The medics have attached an IV line to the fistula and attached ECG leads to her chest. I concentrate on the bleep- bleep sound as the heart trace appears on the monitor. An oxygen mask has been placed over her face. A face that I can hardly recognise. My amazing, beautiful Mother is dying. I feel so helpless and desperate, but more than that, I feel ashamed as I reach into her pocket and retrieve a Valium tablet and surreptitiously pop it into my mouth as I feign a yawn.

The emergency room staff are waiting for us when we arrive. Four members of staff are standing outside of the rear doors of the ambulance and gently transfer Mother onto a trolley, which they proceed to push at full speed through the electronic doors into the hospital, leaving me behind in a state of bewilderment. No one notices me as I walk slowly and aimlessly onwards.

The hospital lights are so bright and dazzling. I feel spaced out. My mind sending false images and messages, as I believe that Mags or someone who resembles her, is walking towards me. I know my mind is playing tricks on me. Amongst the foggy vision of Mags, I think that I can hear her familiar voice, the sound of which I have played over and over again in my mind, like a favourite song from the radio.

Ever since the day at the police station the last time I saw her, I have been desperate to hear her voice, to see her lovely face once more. I never got to say goodbye to her and now I know for sure that I am going insane. Whatever was mixed with the drug is causing me to have visionary and auditory hallucinations. Then I hear it again.

'Alfie. Alfie, it's me Magenta.'

I can't recall what happened next. I only know now because much later, my father told me.

CHAPTER FORTY-FIVE

Alfie

Eighteen months later...

The auditorium is full to bursting with proud families. Each looking towards the stage, where the graduates patiently wait for their name to be called, myself included. I hear my name called as the roar of the clapping quietens down. I climb the five steps up to the stage. I have worked hard for this moment and many sacrifices have been made. This is my moment.

I turn to face the crowd and search for the familiar faces of my family. My heart skips a beat. There they are, on their feet waving frantically, their chests puffed out and tears in their eyes. I wave back at Mother, Father, and Magenta. My life is complete. I feel whole again.

Karma has recorded Mother's life of good deeds and has repaid her with interest. Yet still, she seeks to help others. The lioness in my Mother drove her on to learn more about Asperger's, she is so determined to support other parents and to campaign for more understanding of the condition. With my help, she plans to set up a local support group for families. We hope to raise awareness and help others face the challenges that we had to face alone.

That day at the hospital had been a turning point for me and for my Mother, who was suffering from a myriad of symptoms related to her failing kidneys. The attending registrar said that it was a miracle that she was alive. After my collapse in the hospital of all places, the help I so badly needed was provided. I have often considered if fate had induced me to take the dodgy tablet that resulted in me suffering from anaphylactic shock. I don't remember the breathlessness or the collapse. One thing is for certain, if I had taken it any other time, I would not have survived, away from the swift response of the hospital staff.

I find it hard to believe that the very moment my life could have so swiftly ended, Magenta was at my side. My Mags. My very special and wonderful girl, was there when I needed her the most.

My recovery in terms of the physical symptoms was much speedier than my deteriorating mental health. This took much longer. The diagnosis of Asperger syndrome tipped the balance, something I have now come to terms with. In truth, it makes me who I am. I have learned that I am not neurotypical, I'm wired differently and live in a literal world. This is who I am; brave enough to allow myself to be vulnerable at times, let down my defences and risk rejection. However, more importantly to be seen and loved for who I truly am and not what others think I should be.

When I was out of danger and well enough to visit Mother, Magenta wheeled me to the intensive care unit to see her and put her mind at rest.

I am still in shock at the way my amazing Mags returned into my life, like some kind of miracle. Seeing my Mother so desperately ill, saddened me beyond belief. She looked so tiny and frail. Her skin taut and discoloured over the puffiness of her body. She knew I was there, for she reached her swollen hand towards mine.

Mother licked her cracked, dry lips and tried to talk to me. The effort too much for her. She was at an increased risk of systemic infection; her potassium and phosphorous levels were rising to the level of putting her at risk of toxic poisoning. I leaned in close to kiss her forehead. Mother opened her eyes and gave me a weak smile, there was no fear in her face, it was almost as though she had resigned herself to the fate awaiting her. At that moment, I knew what I had to do. When she stabilised, I arranged a meeting with the nephrologist and after a series of examinations and investigation, it was confirmed that I was a good live donor match. The transplant surgery was arranged to coincide during the Christmas break to minimise any further disruptions to my studies. For me, it was the most special gift I could give to my Mother.

CHAPTER FORTY-SIX

Magenta

It was pure chance that I was working in the emergency room that day. Some would say that it was fate or Karma. Whatever the reason, it reunited me with Alfie. I have thought about him and his mother, Grace, every single day since they saved me and my sisters from the hell we were living through. We were placed in temporary foster care until a permanent home was found. One where we could once again be together.

The loss of our mother and the circumstances surrounding her death were the most painful emotions I have ever felt. Mother knew exactly what father had been doing to me and because of this, I find it difficult to truly feel compassion for her. I knew that she was weak, I was also aware of the cohesive control that my father had over her.

What I don't understand is at what point this began to happen. It must have been a gradual process. Surely, early in their relationship when he began to display unreasonable behaviour, she could have found the strength to walk away and take me and my sisters with her. Sometimes I question what her priorities were? Yes, we had a big house and garden. Mother had beautiful clothes and jewellery, but at what price? She wasn't happy. Even after attending mass and going to confession, she returned with the same haunted look on her face. I find it hard to believe that the Priest listened to her confession, yet no help came our way. No one came to rescue me and my sisters. Maybe one day I will understand, but for now I struggle.

I have never been to visit father in prison and have no intention of doing so. Apparently, he has become more religious than ever, since he has been imprisoned. Does he really think that he can go to confession and be cleansed of his sins? My sisters and I will carry the scars of his debauchery and incestuous behaviour for the rest of our lives.

It was a fortunate day that sent Dorothy and Jack to our aid. They are wonderful foster parents in every way possible, full of love and compassion. My sisters, although still traumatised by my fathers' behaviour and the death of our mother, are gradually blossoming under the love and guidance of Dorothy and Jack. It was Dorothy who found me the hospital placement that subsequently put me directly in the path of Alfie. I have such a great deal to thank them for.

I have continued with my studies and although I never did study law, I chose to do a psychology degree with the Open University enabling me to remain close by my sisters. I have learnt about the many ways of helping to heal the mind. My sisters and I have had cognitive behavioural therapy and regularly practice mindfulness. This is something that I plan to continue with. Alfie has briefly discussed his problems with me, including his diagnosis of Asperger's. He is not ready yet to share all of his concerns, not to me anyway. However, we have plenty of time.

I sincerely hope that my level of understanding of the human mind will be a great asset in my relationship with Alfie, for I fully intend to remain faithfully his.

CHAPTER FORTY-SEVEN

Alfie

I came to a moment in my life, when I needed to do as I had been done by. I know that by giving mother my kidney, I undoubtedly saved her life and yet to me it was a small sacrifice. I knew that Mother had willingly made sacrifices for me, as any loving parent would do. I truly felt a deep need to purge myself of the guilt that I was carrying. No one forced me to get involved with drugs and alcohol. I did that all by myself. The many lies I told have left tiny scars inside of my mind. The psychologist keeps reminding me that as a child, I was not in a position to understand adult relationships and I should not reinforce my pain by ruminating on the issues that trouble me.

On reflection, I realise how ill-equipped the teachers at school were, to deal with my kind of issues. That is something I am currently working on.

Mother and I have started volunteering with the Nottinghamshire branch of the National Autistic Society and we are hoping to raise awareness about Asperger syndrome within schools. I sincerely hope that other young children will be listened to and treated respectfully if they are not neurotypical. Like me, they didn't ask to be born that way. I know that I have had my share of pain and distress, but I cannot lie down and cry or give up. No. But what I can do is to use my hyperawareness to push myself forwards and live my life to the best of my abilities, within my own limitations.

Mags is a tremendous help to me. I always feel at ease with her. She is my soul mate, the love of my life. We are so good together. We share our pain and troubles. We open our hearts and expose our innermost feelings, then find a healing path. Mags, still has her own demons, like me, her battle continues, but we don't let them dominate our lives.

On occasion, I do still consider how mother's life would have been if I had told her about the woman that father was meeting at the playground. When these thoughts pop into my head, I try to remember that times were different, it was Father who made the choice to have an affair. He was the adult. It is no use thinking in terms of the sliding doors theory, the what if's. I was young and struggling with my own tangle of negative feelings, such as my childlike confusion about the way other children treated me.

Surprisingly, I have become much more successful in terms of academia than any of my peers that I went to school with. I feel sure that Kenny would be proud of me. I am learning to let go, to move on from the past and rise above the mistakes I have made. I am making peace with myself. Giving Mother the gift of life, as she had done for me when I was born, has given me absolution.

Dear reader,

Thank you very much for purchasing my novel Love, Secrets, and Absolution. I hope that you enjoyed reading it. If so, please could you spare a few minutes to leave a review on Amazon and/or any other review sites. Thank you - I look forward to reading your feedback.

I love interacting with readers, so please feel free to connect with me via:

Twitter: @K_L_Loveley

Facebook: www.facebook.com/klloveley

Website: www.klloveley.com

Thank you
K.L Loveley

ABOUT K.L LOVELEY

K.L Loveley is a retired nurse, who has seen, heard, and dealt with a wide range of medical, social and family dramas. She has used her nursing experience, along with her excellent people-watching skills to create fascinating characters and intriguing scenarios within her books. She writes contemporary fiction, psychological dramas, and poetry.

Her debut novel *Alice,* was published in February 2017 and the story tackles alcoholism head-on and presents the reader with an empathetic account of a spiralling addiction and the resulting pattern of hopelessness that many fall into.

Her debut poetry collection, *Chameleon Days: The camouflaged and changing emotions of a woman unleashed* is beautifully illustrated by the artist Elvina Dulac.

K.L Loveley lives in Nottinghamshire, England and loves socialising with friends and family. She is an avid reader and enjoys a variety of genres including psychological, thrillers and historical fiction. Her favourite authors include John le Carré, K.L Slater, Marian Keyes, and Philippa Gregory.

Globeflower Books™ is the publishing imprint of

The Globeflower Agency Ltd.

It is our mission to sow the seeds of storytelling
for literature to bloom.

SPECIAL OFFERS

If you would like to be the first to hear about our new
releases, competitions, and receive special book offers, then
please sign up for our e-newsletter at:

www.globeflower.co.uk/e-newsletter

Printed in Great Britain
by Amazon